Light shone in through the windows,
but the space wasn't any less creepy. Old cobwebs hung from the rafters, and dust particles danced in the sunlight. She hoped there wasn't a family of raccoons, or worse, living here. Brynn pushed those thoughts from her mind and kneeled in front of the trunk with the screwdriver. She'd never tried to pick a lock before, but there was a first time for everything.

"If you're set on nosing around, I would rather you used the key. It's under that pile of books."

Brynn jumped to her feet and swung around to face the voice. She gripped tightly to her only weapon, the screwdriver.

There he stood, the same man she saw the other day. "Who are you?" She backed toward the wall, holding the screwdriver in front of her. "You're trespassing."

"No, my dear, you're trespassing. This is my castle. I should be asking you the questions."

Brynn's eyes bugged out as she *really* took a look at him. His image was fading in and out. "No," she said aloud, "it can't be."

"My dear, you don't look well."

"You're a…" She patted her face.

"A what? I'm a what?" His face faded and returned.

"You're a ghost!" Brynn sat on the trunk. The room spun in every direction.

Sebastian's Castle

by

Lisa DeVore

This is a work of fiction. Names, characters, places, and incidents are either the product of the author's imagination or are used fictitiously, and any resemblance to actual persons living or dead, business establishments, events, or locales, is entirely coincidental.

Sebastian's Castle

Contact Information: info@thewildrosepress.com

Cover Art by *Kristian Norris*

The Wild Rose Press, Inc.
PO Box 708
Adams Basin, NY 14410-0708
Visit us at www.thewildrosepress.com

Publishing History
First Fantasy Rose Edition, 2017
Print ISBN 978-1-5092-1332-0
Digital ISBN 978-1-5092-1333-7

Published in the United States of America

Dedication

To my knight in shining armor,
my best friend,
my forever love,
my husband…Lewie DeVore

I hope you enjoy
this story, inspired by
alliance, Ohio's own
"Glamorgan Castle"
Lisa DeVore

Chapter One

Brynn Austin sat on the window seat of her Brooklyn brownstone. She peered down at a couple strolling down the sidewalk hand in hand, oblivious to anything, but each other. Brynn sighed at what used to be, what could have been.

Resting on her lap was a folded American flag, the one that draped across her husband's casket over a year ago. It didn't feel like a year ago. Actually, it seemed more like yesterday her husband's partner had been on the other side of the door to give her the news that changed her life.

Snow floated silently to the ground outside the window. The *For Sale* sign attached to the rod-iron fence now said *Sold.* The realtor had come by this morning to give her the good news. Only now, she was second-guessing herself.

Brynn glanced over at Romeo, her cat. "Who leaves a perfectly good job to buy a castle in Connecticut?" And a run-down castle at that.

Boxes surrounded her throughout the modest sized living room. She gently tucked the flag into a special box of Nate's things. How did it come to this—his life in a cardboard box? His bravery had gotten him a Medal of Valor. A piece of hardware meant nothing without him. She sighed, closed the box, and taped it shut. Too bad she couldn't do that with the memories that haunted her.

Nathaniel Austin was two weeks past his thirtieth birthday when he was shot and killed during an undercover operation involving a drug and weapons ring. Nate had saved the life of Apollo Banks, a known gang leader, on a cold autumn day over a year ago. That act would eventually lead to Nate's death, and change her life forever.

The NYC Police Department took full advantage of Nate's new standing. Apollo had no idea Nate was a police officer that fateful day, walking from the subway station. Another gang leader had pulled a gun on Apollo, and Nate saw it first. He tackled the guy with the gun and won himself into an inside operation. Brynn knew about his undercover work and wasn't a fan, but he assured her it was all very safe. If only she could rewind the past and have a do-over.

The night sky descended sometime during her trip down memory lane. She secured two more boxes when the buzzer rang by her door. Brynn peeked out and saw her longtime friend standing there with a pizza box. God, she was going to miss her. She opened the door with a smile.

"I brought pizza, because I know you didn't eat."

"What's in the bag?" Brynn craned her neck.

"Maybe a little wine to get me through the goodbyes." Lola had been her friend since the first grade, and until recently, co-workers. Brynn was going to need the wine too.

"I have the fine china in here." She passed Lola a foam plate and a disposable cup. Everything was packed.

"Don't dirty anything on my account. I'll eat it out

of the box. I'm starved."

"So, how was work without me?" Brynn grabbed napkins on her way out of the kitchen.

"Boring. I still can't believe you're going through with this. Don't get me wrong. It takes guts. I just wonder about the timing."

The recent purchase of a late nineteenth-century castle left Brynn wondering about her own sanity. When would be the right time? All she had left of Nate was some mementos, a flag, and a dream. Waiting would accomplish nothing—only the possibility of losing out on this Connecticut landmark. "Nate would want me to go through with it. This was our dream."

"Yeah, I know. I get it. I'm gonna miss you, that's all."

"I'm not moving across the country. Only a few hours away. You can visit anytime. I can always use help with the renovations."

Most of the time Brynn couldn't believe she was doing this either. She'd had a great job as an interior designer, but the city was fast paced—exhausting at times. And with Nate's high stress job, life was flying by. She and Nate had looked at this castle fourteen months ago and envisioned a quieter, simpler life—a life where she didn't have to worry about her husband being shot at, and where they could slow down the hands on the clock. They longed for a safe place to raise a family. He had been so pumped at the idea of renovating this to a bed and breakfast. They had saved and scrimped for years, and worked all the overtime they could get their hands on. When they pulled up to the castle that sunny day, they immediately knew this was their dream come true. Then the dream had died with a gunshot wound to the head.

When Brynn finally crawled out of her despair and realized she had no choice but to go on without him, she checked with her realtor about the castle. It was still available. Brynn handed over their life savings and signed on the dotted line. She sat in her car and sobbed until there were no tears left. A sense of calm settled over her, and she let herself believe Nate was with her, guiding her. Yes, she would do this…for both of them. Tomorrow she and Romeo would be moving to Mystic, Connecticut, and Sebastian's Castle to start a new chapter.

"Did I show you the pictures I took the last time I visited?" Brynn rooted through her purse and grabbed her phone. She pulled up about ten snapshots and handed it over to Lola. She watched her eyebrows pull down and a frown cross her face. "What do you think?"

She handed the phone back to Brynn. "Well…it's, umm…a fixer-upper."

Brynn laughed. "It is that."

"So, what do you do first? I wouldn't even know where to begin."

"Electricity," Brynn stated evenly.

"You're kidding, right?" She paused for a response, but got nothing. "You're going to live there without electricity? I'd imagine that place gets a little chilly this time of the year."

"The electrician and the general contractor are meeting me there tomorrow. I'm staying in a nearby hotel until I have the necessities."

Lola wiped her mouth and took a swig of wine. "I have to admit you had me worried."

"Don't look so skeptical. I can do this. I need to do

this. I'm existing here—going through the motions, you know? It'll give me something positive to focus on, instead of all I've lost."

Brynn topped off her red cup after Lola departed, then pulled a small note pad from her purse, and listed all the things she wanted to accomplish in order of importance.

Romeo climbed up on her lap, drawing her attention away from her list. He purred with satisfaction as she scratched his neck. She tried to picture him moving around the castle. He could be lost for days in such a huge place. Was she doing the right thing?

She'd be on the road at the crack of dawn. The movers would arrive the following day to put what she wasn't taking into storage. Her realtor had agreed to oversee the process. She wouldn't have to be there when they carried her life out the door. There was no turning back.

She glanced around one last time before turning in. Tears welled up despite her best effort to be strong—the way Nate would want her to be. There were so many memories here, and most of them revolved around her late husband. They had forgone the huge wedding and instead chose to purchase a home. The guilt crept into her thoughts. This new adventure was one he wanted too. She would be living it for the both of them. But closing the door on this place was like leaving him behind. There was no way around the sadness. She had to go through it.

Chapter Two

Brynn drove through the gates and down the long, tree-lined lane. The tires of her car crunched over the snow-covered brick. Her heart rate quickened as she grew closer to the porte-cochere, or in simpler terms, a covered carriage gate. The entry had left an impression on her. She could picture the carriages pulling up with ladies and gents dressed in their finery, and almost hear the hooves against brick, and the neighing of the horses.

She stopped inside the enclosure and turned off the engine. The silence in the car was deafening. All her emotions rose to the surface. Could she handle this renovation by herself? She was on her own in a drafty old castle. Romeo grumbled from the backseat in protest. Okay. She wasn't completely alone.

Digging in her purse, she found the key to her future…for better or worse. "Are you ready to see your new home, Romeo?"

She climbed out of the car and pulled the cat carrier from the back. Wide, gray, marble steps leading to the loggia waited in front of her. Brynn crossed to the entrance and stopped to admire the beautiful wood of the door. Deep brown in color, the style was medieval. It certainly fit a castle but could use a fresh coat of stain.

Brynn nudged the door open. It protested with a loud moan, reminding her of every horror film she ever watched—that scene viewed through a web of fingers, a rapid heartbeat, and warnings from the audience to run the other way. Her stomach dropped to her kneecaps. She ignored the argument in her head to retreat to her car and entered the long hall. The flashlight she had tucked in her coat pocket came to life, and so did that inner voice warning caution. She decided to wait for the electrician and contractor right where she stood. It wasn't that she was afraid of ghosts. It was the living people that made her nervous, and not knowing if any of them were creeping around her castle.

Brynn glanced at her watch. She had twenty minutes before they were to meet. No reason to stand in a cold, drafty hallway. She grabbed the cat and headed for the car. She convinced herself it was for the heat. The shadows at the end of the hall had nothing to do with her decision. Her eyes nervously scanned the outside of the castle while she waited in the safety of her car. Something wasn't right. She expected to see a face staring out one of those large windows. The goose bumps spread across her skin.

A truck pulled up behind her. The door swung open, and she could make out *Maddox Construction* across it. Brynn had only talked to Mr. Maddox on the phone. He had come highly recommended in the area. He was pleasant and seemed to know what he was talking about. Nate had been the one good at judging character. She hoped she'd made the right decision in hiring him.

She watched from the mirror, not able to make out his face. "Well, Romeo, let's get this show on the road." Brynn pulled on her gloves and lowered her hat before stepping out of her car. She wasn't expecting the man who exited the truck. If she had to guess, he was in his early thirties. With his credentials, she anticipated someone older. He was bundled up, but his jaw-dropping smile couldn't be missed.

He moved toward her and reached out his hand. "Mrs. Austin? Jaxson Maddox. Pleased to finally meet you."

She returned the smile. "Likewise. I could ask you inside, but I'm afraid it's freezing in there too." The wind whipped around them. "Dark too."

"I have a flashlight in the truck that should do the trick."

While he was retrieving the flashlight, Brynn returned to her car and ran the engine, so Romeo didn't freeze. She hit the alarm on her spare key and shoved it in her pocket. The added bonus would be getting into a warm car at the end of the meeting.

"Shall we?" he asked.

Brynn led the way to the door, inserted the key into the lock, and turned the knob. She stepped in and moved to the side for him to enter. All kinds of thoughts rushed through her head. He could be a nut case, or there could be a nut case hiding in here…or both. The joys of being married to a cop. Paranoia.

She broke the silence. "I didn't venture too far in when I arrived. It's sat empty for so long. I was afraid of what I might find, or who."

"Understandable." He shined the light down the long hallway toward the rotunda that sold her and Nate. The light cast an eerie shadow. Very different from the sunny day they visited.

"Should we wait for the electrician?" she asked as he moved down the hall.

"We'll stick around here, so he can find us." He cast light up into the dome. "This is a huge project. You and your husband are brave to take it on."

She fought back tears. "I'm widowed."

"I'm sorry. I didn't realize. I guess I stuck my foot in my mouth. You're awfully young to be alone."

"No need to apologize. We never covered that in our conversations. My husband was NYPD. He died on the job."

"Man, that's tough."

She cleared her throat. "We were looking at this place just before he died. It's been a dream of ours to open a bed and breakfast. I didn't want to let the dream die with him. I have to accomplish this for the both of us."

"I promise to do what I can to make that happen."

The door flung open with a rush of wind following. "Anyone in here?"

Mr. Maddox answered. "Down here, Mike."

Another flashlight flipped on. "Mrs. Austin, Jax…" He addressed them. "I'm sorry I'm late. I was going over some plans at the office and lost track of time. I'm good at what I do, but not so good with the clock."

Brynn smiled. She immediately liked him and was at ease. Mr. Johansson was an older gentleman and was recommended by the contractor. "That's fine. We only arrived ourselves."

"This is going to be a big project, Mike. You onboard?"

"Never been afraid of a challenge. And this is a good cause. I'd like to see this place up and running again."

Brynn shoved her hands deep into her pockets. "I

need heat and lights as soon as possible. I'll be staying down the road at the inn until I can stay here."

"Why don't you climb in that heated car of yours?" Mike suggested. "We'll poke around and see what's on the agenda first."

She shivered. "If you don't mind I'd like to follow along. I might as well see the damage first hand."

"It's your rodeo, little lady. Let me grab my clipboard out of the truck."

That left her alone with Jaxson Maddox.

He spoke out of the blue. "Do you have plans for dinner?"

"Oh, I…" she stammered. "I mean, that's nice of you, but you don't have to."

His light gleamed across the ceiling. "I know I don't have to. I want to. You're new to the area, and it would be easier talking over a cheeseburger than shivering in here."

Good thing he couldn't see the different shades of red her face was turning. She had jumped to the conclusion he was asking her out on a date. But it would be a business meeting. She could live with that. "Okay. But would you mind giving me an hour or so? I need to check in to the hotel and drop Romeo off."

"Romeo? You're welcome to bring him with you."

"Romeo's my cat."

"Oh." He laughed. She envisioned the smile she witnessed when he stepped out of his truck. "Sure. I'd like to run home and grab a shower. Get the work day off of me. What hotel are you staying at? I'll pick you up."

"I could meet you there." More cop paranoia.

"I promise I'm safe."

"I'm sorry. I'm naturally cautious. I'm at The Wharf."

"That's a great place. You'll like it. I did some work there. The view's really something."

"That's a relief. They can make anything look good on line."

"Sorry to keep you kids waiting. Couldn't find a damned pencil."

With flashlights ablaze, they were on their way. Nate should have been there by her side, asking the questions. He was the one who could fix anything. She pushed the anger aside. One day Apollo Banks would pay for what he did to her life, but right now she had to live hers until that day came.

"Mrs. Austin, watch your step." Jaxson cradled her elbow as she stepped over a loose board.

She could see his face in the dim lighting. "Thank you."

"Sure. Careful, right in front of us." He hadn't let go of her arm.

He was being polite, and that made her uncomfortable. The moment passed, and for the next half hour, she followed them as they measured, discussed, and planned their level of attack.

"This is going to be an exciting project, but a huge one. You do understand the amount of work that's involved?" Jaxson asked.

"I'm aware. My husband was more knowledgeable than I am, but we had talked at length about what it would need to bring it back. As an interior decorator, I'm not totally clueless. If you're worried about funding, I'm good. We had money saved..." She attempted to keep her voice even. "...and I have his life insurance."

"Of course, money's part of it. Most people don't understand the cost adds up, and there's always unforseens—the things we won't know about until we get into the bones of the project. And there's the time factor too. This isn't going to be a weekend job, and we'll be under your feet for a while."

Brynn liked Mr. Maddox's direct manner. "I understand. I was in a similar line of work. Although, my end was more visionary, and I left the mechanics to the construction wizards, I understand the add-on costs. I'm committed to this."

Mr. Johansson chimed in. "Well then, I'll be working on that permit, so I can get started."

Brynn clutched at the extra key in her pocket—the one that was supposed to be Nate's. She handed it off to Jax, and they agreed on a safe place to keep it.

"Good enough. I'll be on my way. The missus hates when I'm late to supper."

"You're a lucky man, Mike. I'll see you tomorrow." Jaxson focused his attention on Brynn. "I'll be by to pick you up, say, around seven?"

"That's really not necessary. I could meet you…"

"What's your room number?"

Obviously, she was making too big a deal out of his generosity. "I'll be in room six. I haven't been there yet, so I don't know exactly where it is."

"I'll find you." He accompanied her to her car and waited until she was behind the wheel.

"Thank you, again, Mr. Maddox."

"It's just Jax, and I haven't done anything yet."

Did he just wink at her? And what did he mean by it? Was he flirting? She hoped not. She would assume he was being kind—an attempt to lighten the mood. Brynn forced a smile and shut the door, waved, and headed back down the lane. Her thoughts were all over the place, but mostly with Nathaniel Austin, and why he had to leave her.

Chapter Three

Brynn traveled the short distance to the inn. The inviting call of a warm shower hurried her movements to the front desk. If the greeting was any indication, this was the perfect place to stay. A staff member explained everything—from parking, breakfast, and places to see. Although, she wouldn't have much time for sightseeing.

"Thank you so much for allowing me to bring my cat. I promise you won't even know he's here."

"When you told us about your husband, well, we wanted to be a part of your new start. If there's anything you need, please let us know. Your room's on the second floor."

Brynn grabbed her overnight bag and Romeo. She slipped the room key into the lock and turned the knob. The giant windows grabbed her attention. The day was gloomy, and light snow fell…a perfect day for the fireplace in the room. She crossed to the bed where she placed the cat carrier.

"Here you go." She opened the door to her traveling companion. He ambled out slowly and took a long, drawn out stretch.

Brynn stood at the windows overlooking the river. How she wished Nate were here. This would have been the perfect place for an anniversary get-a-way. There would be no more anniversaries for them. She sighed and attempted to draw her attention away from her morbid thoughts by peeking into the bathroom.

A half hour of settling in passed before she stepped into the shower. The travel and worries of the day slid down the drain. She grabbed a pair of jeans and a cream cable-knit sweater. She accessorized with a scarf and necessary suede boots.

She glanced at her watch just as a knock echoed through the room. Romeo ran under the bed. "A watch-cat you are not." She opened the door and wasn't prepared for what was on the other side. Apparently, the winter garb had hidden Mr. Maddox's drop-dead gorgeous self.

"Mr. Maddox, come in. I'll just grab my coat."

"It's Jax. We're going to be spending a lot of time together, and Mr. Maddox is a little formal, don't you think?"

"Only if you call me Brynn." He took the coat from her hands and held it open for her. "And you have manners."

"At times."

A change of subject was desperately needed. "So, where are we eating?"

"I thought we'd go to the pub. They have a great menu."

"That sounds perfect. I'm starved."

"Are you opposed to walking? It's not far."

"I don't mind at all. Might help me burn off some of this restless energy."

They moved through the streets of Mystic until they reached the front door of their destination. Jax opened the door, and she walked into a place she immediately knew she would be spending a lot of her time.

"Let's sit over here by the fireplace," he suggested.

Brynn slipped off her coat and soaked in the scenery. The fire crackled and popped, putting off heat she craved after their walk here. In another time, she would have appreciated the romantic surroundings. She pushed aside the emotion rising to the surface and once again focused elsewhere.

A waitress took their drink order moments after they settled in. Jax ordered a beer, and she, an Irish coffee. They sat in silence while they looked over the menu.

"Everything looks delicious. What do you suggest?"

"I always get a burger. Guess you could say I'm in a rut." There was the smile again that told her he was a nice man.

"Okay. A burger it is."

"Are you ready to order?" the waitress asked.

"Brynn?"

"I am." The delicious aromas wafting around set her stomach grumbling in protest.

"Will this be one bill or two?"

"One." Jax replied without missing a beat.

"Two." This would not be a date.

"Ignore her. I'm going to be rude and order first, so she can't argue. I'll take a burger with the works and some fries. "

"And what can I get you?"

"Same. Thank you." Brynn waited until the waitress left the table before saying, "I don't expect you to pay. This isn't a date."

"No, Brynn, it's a write-off." He attempted humor,

but all she could do was fidget with her napkin. "I know this must be tough on you. How long since he passed?"

"A little over a year." The sadness in her voice was even obvious to her.

"He was a lucky guy. I can tell you loved him a lot."

"It's hard going on without him. Every day I wake up, hoping it's some kind of nightmare, but it's not. It's my reality."

"What happened? If you don't want to talk about it, I understand."

For some reason, with him, she didn't mind. "An undercover operation went bad."

"Did they get the person who did it?"

"No. The police know. I know. But they don't have any proof."

Jax took a swig of his beer. "Well, hopefully, you can make a new start here. It's a great place to live. The summers are my favorite. Do you like boating?"

"I've never been, unless you count the Staten Island Ferry."

"You'll find there's a lot to do here. So…getting down to business. Do you have any ideas on how you want to tackle this project? What's your order of importance?"

"The first step would be the electrical. I can't see two feet in front of me to see what I'm up against. Naturally, the heating and plumbing would be my next priority. I think living there will give me a better idea of how I want the flow of rooms."

"It needs a great deal of work. Are you ready to live in a construction zone?"

The doubt on his face gave her pause. "I know it's

not going to be easy. I'll figure out where I want my private quarters, and we'll tackle that first."

"You said you're an interior designer?"

"I was. Back in New York." So much had changed.

"I know we've touched on this, but I want to make sure you understand this won't happen overnight. People tend to think I can snap my fingers and have a job done in a week."

"I understand. My husband knew more about construction, but I have a general knowledge. I've helped many clients through restorations and additions. I promise to give you two weeks."

He chuckled. The tense muscles eased, and she found she actually enjoyed his company.

"Do you know the history of the castle?" he asked.

"I know it was built in 1898 by a wealthy shipbuilder, but I really haven't gotten too far into its history."

He grinned.

"What? Are you going to tell me it's haunted?"

"Well, as a matter of fact…"

"Come on, Jax. You're not going to tell me you believe in ghosts?"

"You don't?"

"I suppose I never thought about it, but I'd have to go with 'not really'."

"Rumor has it the castle has sat empty all these years because it's haunted by the original owner."

"You don't seem the type to believe in urban legends."

He laughed. "You're right. But it might be a good marketing tool for your bed and breakfast."

"And it might scare people off."

He shook his head. "No, ghosts are in now. Didn't you know that?"

At that moment, the waitress brought their dinners. Over the next hour, they conversed over her plans for the castle, local shops, and her former job. There was no more talk about ghosts, friendly, or otherwise.

Jax and Brynn exited the pub and were greeted with a steady snowfall. She barely made it out the door when she slipped on an icy spot. Jax grabbed her arm, steadying her.

"I'm sorry. I guess I should have packed boots that were more practical, and less stylish."

"Ice is ice." He held out his arm. "Hold on to me."

Brynn stopped and faced him. "I wouldn't want people to get the wrong idea."

"Look around. There aren't many people out here to get the wrong idea."

He was right. Overreacting was fast becoming her norm. She looped her arm through his. Her stomach dropped at the contact.

Why did she feel like she was cheating on Nate?

Chapter Four

Jax opened the door to the lobby of her temporary home and motioned for her to precede him. She pulled off her gloves and rubbed her hands together. "Thanks for the burger. I appreciate you showing the pub to me." How many ways could you say *awkward*?

"My pleasure. Mike and I'll get the permits in motion. Shouldn't be too long before we can get started. I'll give you a call."

"Thank you." She forced a smile. Her nerves overtook her good sense. She bit down on her lip and headed for the stairs. Should she have said something else? God, she must look like an idiot.

"Brynn?"

She stopped on the first step and turned. "Yeah?"

"If you need anything. Call me."

She nodded but couldn't respond. Did she see pity in his expression? Her nose stung, warning her of tears forthcoming. She continued up the steps without looking back, opened the door, stepped in, and leaned against the door. The dam burst. His offer reinforced what she already knew. She had no one. Jax was a nice man, but he could never be Nate. No one could. Whatever happened in her future, she would have to deal with it alone.

Brynn swiped at her face, still leaning against the door, when Romeo made his appearance and jumped on the bed. She laughed through her tears. "Where were you hiding, you big chicken?" He was always good for a distraction.

She moved across the room to the sitting area and turned on another light. She reached for the cord to shut the blinds and was caught up in the beauty outside her window. The glow from the lamp posts reflected off each snowflake that fell gracefully to the ground. With a heavy heart, she closed herself off from the scene outside.

Brynn lowered herself onto the navy blue couch and noticed a stack of wood next to the fireplace. The idea of some extra heat sounded heavenly. Within ten minutes the fire blazed orange, and her mind wandered. Memories with Nate were still bittersweet. She wanted so much for him to be here, and each morning she started the day without him was a cruel reminder that part of her life was over. Her only defense against the thoughts that clouded her days was to keep busy.

What better way than searching for the castle ghost? Brynn changed into comfy clothes and placed her computer on the coffee table in front of the fire. She typed into the search engine *Sebastian Morgan castle* and to her surprise quite a few choices appeared before her. She clicked the first entry and skimmed the information, going on to the second.

It would seem Sebastian Morgan wasn't without controversy. Brynn settled in and read.

Sebastian Morgan started a small ship building business with longtime friend, Jonathan Hammond. The business partners, without help, built their first whaling boat and sold it for a small profit. His partner decided the work too intense for the small amount they profited, so Sebastian purchased his partner's share of the company. Knowing he couldn't build boats single-handedly, he hired on two employees. The company grew and so did the boats. He paid a fair wage but demanded much from his employees. For the most part, his workers appeared loyal.

Jonathan Hammond learned of his former partner's success and returned to Mystic seeking compensation. When Morgan refused his outrageous demands and sent him packing, Hammond vowed his revenge.

"Well, what do you know, Romeo? We have ourselves more history than we imagined." She continued to read with excitement.

Jonathan Hammond returned to Mystic, where he opened a rival business, stole Morgan's employees with the promise of higher wages and bonuses for work completed ahead of deadline. The pushing and pulling continued between the adversaries, one always trying to outdo the other.

In 1898, Sebastian Morgan began construction of a castle that would rival those of Europe. Anything to make the residents of Mystic forget the mansion built by Hammond to show off his success.

During construction, Sebastian married the town's most beautiful lady of high society, Helena Baldridge. Her family spent their summers in Connecticut. Helena's father was a wealthy New York attorney. Sebastian thought this a great match. Not only would he have a beautiful wife, but an attorney at the ready.

That was until Jonathan Hammond set his sights on Sebastian's wife. Although dashing, Sebastian's looks did not compare to the handsome Mr. Hammond.

They attended the same society parties, many of which Sebastian refused to grace. Helena loved the parties and entertaining. Rumors began to swirl as Mr. Hammond and Mrs. Morgan were mentioned in the gossip columns dancing the night away. It is not known if her actions were a cry for attention from her husband whose focus was centered on building his business and staying ahead of the competition.

Mr. Morgan made an unexpected appearance at a party his wife was attending. His suspicions were verified when he witnessed his wife on the arm of his rival. Heated words were exchanged in front of the guests before Mr. Morgan rather roughly escorted his wife from the premises. Soon after, she was reported missing, and so there begins the mystery of what happened to Helena Baldridge Morgan?

Brynn clicked another link about the mystery, the story near the same. She jumped when her cell phone rang across the room. She expected to see Lola's name on the screen, but she found *Maddox Construction* flashing at her instead. She thought about letting it ring, but decided against it.

"Hello."

"Hey, Brynn. Did I wake you?"

She looked at the clock. Had she really been engrossed in Sebastian Morgan's life that long?

"No, I've been reading about Sebastian Morgan and lost track of time."

"So, you're beginning to believe in ghosts?" he asked, his voice full of amusement.

"I didn't say that. Actually, I was reading about the living man. He had quite a life story."

"What did you find out?"

Surely, he didn't call about this. "I would think a local, like you, would know all about it."

"Not quite a local. I've lived here about ten years. I only know what I've heard here and there."

Surprising. She would have pegged him for a local. "Well, Mr. Sebastian Morgan had a bit of feud with a friend-turned-business partner-turned enemy. His wife may, or may not, have had an affair with said enemy. Then she disappeared. I haven't found out what happened to him after that. Although, I gather he was under suspicion for her disappearance."

"You don't say? A story like that could drum up business if promoted."

"I'm sorry I side-tracked you. What can I help you with?"

He paused for a few seconds before speaking. "I wanted to ask if you wanted to ride along for the permits tomorrow morning. In case we need something," he added quickly.

Brynn couldn't imagine what they would need. "I suppose I can. It's not like my schedule's full."

"Good. How about I pick you up around eight, and we can stop for breakfast?"

"You really don't have to babysit me, Mr. Maddox."

"Why won't you call me Jax?" Her stomach flipped.

"We just met." Her mind rolled with her real thoughts. He was attractive, single, and she needed to keep her distance. She wasn't ready for anything. Nate still held her heart.

"For the record, I'm not babysitting. I remember what it's like to be new in town. And I like your company."

"I…" She wasn't sure how to say what was on her mind.

"What? My ego can handle it if you don't want to have breakfast with me."

"It's not that. I like your company too. I'm not over my husband." There she said it.

"I understand, Brynn. Do you have room in your life for a friend?"

She smiled at that. "I do. I'm in short supply."

"Yeah, well, me too. I work too much. So, we're on for breakfast?"

"Yes, breakfast and permits."

"I can take you by the library, and you could do some research on your Mr. Morgan."

Brynn liked the idea. "Do you think they would have information about him?"

"Worth a try. They have a room devoted to local history. The castle's a big part of that. It may have sat empty for a while, but the locals still consider it a landmark."

"I wonder if they'd have pictures of it back in the day?" Her excitement grew. "I'd like to restore it to its glory days. It would be great if I could see the décor of the time."

"Have you checked the attic?"

"For?"

"I've found a lot of stuff in these old places, left behind by previous owners. Maybe there are some pictures, or some antique furniture."

She hadn't thought of that possibility. "That's an idea, but I'm not going up there alone."

"Ahh," he teased, "afraid of ghosts?"

"More like wild animals and insane people."

He laughed. "How about if I go up with you and protect you from the squirrels?"

A warm feeling passed over her, suddenly changing to guilt. She longed for that feeling of protection again, but it should be her husband protecting her.

"Brynn?"

"Yeah, I'm here." She pushed against her gut reaction. She would take his offer for the good of the project. "Maybe we can squeeze that in tomorrow too?"

"I look forward to it. Goodnight, Brynn."

"Goodnight, Jax. Thank you." She ended the conversation with trembling hands. She shouldn't look forward to seeing him, but she did. Her heart broke for the love she lost. The sick feeling in the pit of her stomach told her there was no room for anything, but friendship, with Jax Maddox. She would accept friendship, nothing else, but it would be nice to have a friend to talk to.

Chapter Five

As promised, Jax showed up bright and early. They grabbed a quick breakfast at the local diner, then handled the red tape needed to begin work.

"The library, or treasure hunting first?" Jax asked.

"Treasure hunting. It's a great idea. I can go to the library later."

Jax shifted his truck in gear and headed for the castle. Her excitement grew when they turned onto the tree-lined lane covered in snow. The scene was picture perfect. The gray marble glistened in the sunlight. It didn't look so scary at the moment.

The snow crunched under the tires of Jax's four-wheel drive truck. He slowed to a stop at the carriage entrance. Brynn reached into her purse for her key.

"Ready?"

She smiled, not able to contain the excitement of possibilities. She had to admit, having someone with her took away the jitters. "Thanks for coming with me."

"Happy to. Let's get in there and see if we can find anything interesting."

The sudden burst of cold took Brynn's breath away. The sun was definitely deceiving. She rushed up to the door and gained entry. The hallway was brighter today with the sunshine, but not much warmer. "How soon do you think before we have heat?"

Jax closed the door behind him. "At least a couple

of weeks. Everything's outdated and not much up to code. Heat is the priority."

Brynn stopped at the sound—a slamming door from somewhere upstairs. Her eyes widened. "Did you hear that?"

"How could I not? Stay here. I'll check it out."

"Don't go up there."

"It's probably a draft." He pulled a small pistol from under his coat.

"You need *that* for a draft?"

"It's legal. Stay here."

Naturally, she didn't listen. She wasn't going to be the door greeter if someone took the back stairs. She stayed behind him, but if he stopped suddenly, she would run right into him.

He looked over his shoulder at her and whispered, "I told you to stay."

"I'm not a dog," she said impatiently.

"Stay close then." He didn't have to tell her that.

They inched down the hall, carefully stopping before each door before moving on. He looked around the corner into the rotunda, and motioned her forward, toward the grand staircase.

Brynn swallowed. She grabbed his coat and stopped him. Someone was walking up there. She pointed up the stairs, and he nodded. They kept close to the inside wall as they ascended. He hesitated when they reached the top. Staying out of sight from any possible intruders, he pulled the flashlight from his pocket and illuminated the upper level of the rotunda. They saw nothing and moved forward. He shined the light on the doors that circled the upper level. Only one was closed. He moved toward that door.

"Maybe we should call the police," she whispered.

"Probably should." But he continued toward the door, stopping beside it. Jax grabbed the knob and pushed the door open and waited momentarily, out of the line of fire. With the pistol poised, he cautiously peeked his head around the corner and moved the light around the room. "All clear. I want you to stay here. I'm going to check the other rooms."

Brynn kept her back to the wall, watching Jax go from room to room until he was by her side again. "There's no one up here."

"You're sure? Maybe they went down the back steps." She shoved her shaking hands into her coat pockets.

"We would have heard them. My money's on a drafty old house."

"I hope you're right." She wasn't convinced.

"We'll check the windows and doors before we leave. Since we're up here, you ready to check out the attic?"

Her enthusiasm waned after the scare, but she had to suck it up. After all, this was going to be her home. She couldn't get all freaked every time she heard a noise. "Right. The attic. It's this way."

Brynn led him down a long hallway. There was a door that led to the servants' quarters, right before the upstairs library. She reached for the doorknob and glanced over her shoulder.

"You want me to go first." He directed a teasing grin toward her.

"If you don't mind. You're armed."

"About that…"

"It's okay. My husband was a cop. There's no need

for an explanation. I'm actually glad you have it."

"Good." He opened the door, turned left, and climbed the creaky staircase. There was ample natural lighting from the sunshine filtering through a window on the landing. No flashlight was needed.

Brynn gasped as they reached the top. A slow smile spread across her face. "Furniture," she announced.

Jax returned the smile. "Pay dirt, baby."

Brynn ran her hand across a lovely, ornate red velvet couch covered in dust. If she had to guess, it was original to the house. She turned and soaked in every piece around her, from wooden chairs, tables…and then she saw it—an old trunk. She rushed over.

She attempted to open it. "It's locked," she said with frustration.

"I have a crow bar in the truck."

"You're not serious."

"Okay. I'm not serious. Don't you want to see what's inside?"

"Well, yeah, but I don't want to destroy it. Can't you pick the lock?"

"I'm a contractor, not a jewel thief. Maybe I have something in the truck. I could try to pry it open."

"There could be a key." She glanced around the attic.

"Do you really think we'll find a key in this mess?"

"I can't destroy it. There has to be something on the internet about locks without keys." She kneeled down and inspected it.

"Yeah. I think it's *Safe Breaking 101*."

"Funny." She pulled her phone out and took some pictures of the trunk and the furniture. "I bet I could reuse some of this furniture." The wheels turned in her mind.

"If we can get that old thing open there might be pictures, or documents, that could help you nail down the history."

"I wish it wasn't locked." She sighed. Destroying antiques wasn't her thing though. "There has to be a way to…" She stopped mid-sentence at the sound of voices below. "Mike and the guys must be here." Jax descended the stairs, and Brynn followed, but when they reached the bottom all was quiet and no one was around.

Brynn crossed her arms in front of her. "Jax, I'm officially freaked."

"There has to be a reasonable explanation," he assured her. "Maybe they went outside to check something."

"Or I just bought myself a haunted castle."

"I thought you didn't believe in ghosts? It's dark and cold in here. Plenty of shadows to make the imagination run wild. You still want to go to the library?"

"Please. You can drop me off, and I'll walk back to the inn. I'm not sure how long I'll be there."

He hesitated. "I wouldn't feel right leaving you there."

"I'm not your responsibility. Plenty of people walk around here. I'll be fine."

His expression turned grim. "Dinner then?"

"I think I'm going to order one of those famous Mystic pizzas and stay in tonight, but thanks."

He nodded. "Well, if you get bored call me."

"I have plenty to work on. I have all kinds of plans

to go over for the castle."

"Maybe, I'll use the time to learn how to pick a lock."

She laughed. "Thanks, Jax. I appreciate the company today. I can't imagine what I would've done if I'd heard that door slam while I was on my own. I'd probably still be running."

They walked to the truck, and there was no sign of Mr. Johannson or anyone else for that matter. Brynn stopped and looked to an upstairs window.

"What's the matter?"

"You ever feel like you're being watched?" She squinted at the sunshine in her face.

His silence did nothing for her nerves. She glanced his way. He was looking up too.

Jax opened the truck door. "We're caught up in the ghost story thing, that's all. Let's get going."

"I suppose you're right."

As he pulled around the circle, she would have sworn she saw a figure in the window she had concentrated on. She faced forward. *Brynn Austin, you do not believe in ghosts.*

Chapter Six

He watched them drive away. Would these people never give up? He'd scare one group out and another followed. The parade of people was getting tiresome. This was his house. Who did these people think they were, wondering around here poking through his things? If they wanted to believe he was a ghost he could deal with that. He just wanted to be left alone. Time to dig out the old chains…

****

Jax dropped off Brynn at the entrance to the library. She found the reference desk with little trouble, and an older lady with graying hair sat behind the desk.

"May I help you?" Her pleasant face put Brynn at ease.

"Yes, thank you. I've purchased Sebastian's Castle, and I'm looking for some information."

"About his ghost?"

The comment surprised Brynn a bit, but she breezed by the question. "I'm more interested in the history. Maybe old pictures, descriptions of the building…anything to help me in the restoration process."

"Oh, I'm sorry. Most people want to know if it's haunted. I believe we may have some things in our Mystic room that might assist you."

"Mystic room?"

"We have a room that contains only local history. You can't check anything out, but I'd be glad to make copies of anything that interests you." She paused. "Are you sure you're not interested in the ghost?"

"Well, I haven't run into any ghosts yet." Or had she?

"Several people have purchased the old place, but none stayed around long enough to do anything. One couple packed up and moved in the middle of the night."

Brynn thought back to the door slamming and the conversations of people that didn't exist. "I'm sure it was overactive imaginations."

"Maybe so," the librarian agreed, but her tone told Brynn she wasn't convinced. "Follow me," she directed.

She unlocked and opened the door to a room full of books and newspapers. She could smell the history in here. "This is great. How long do I have to look around?"

"We close at five, but give me time to make the copies you need. Over here is an article…" She shuffled through some papers. "Here it is. This was written during the hundredth anniversary. I believe there's some background on Sebastian Morgan, the builders, and some pictures of the interior."

"Perfect. Thank you."

"Let me know if you need any help." She exited, leaving Brynn to her research.

She glanced at the clock and was surprised at the time. She had spent the entire afternoon sifting through articles and pictures. She gathered her stack to be copied and headed to the reference desk. She had only skimmed through most of the information and looked forward to really checking them out back at her room.

Her phone buzzed. "Hello, Jax."

"You have me on caller ID?"

"You caught me. What's up?"

"I'm sitting outside the library with a famous pizza, and no one to eat it with. How about a ride and a free meal?"

Brynn smiled despite the uneasy feeling. Every time he asked her to do something, thoughts of Nate crept in, and so did the guilt. Jax swore he was offering his friendship, so why did her stomach churn every time he suggested a casual meeting?

A thought crossed her mind. "How did you know I was still here? Be honest. You're hiding behind one of the bookshelves." Brynn glanced around.

"No hiding, just good instincts. I figured you'd get wrapped up and forget the time. I confess I have an ulterior motive."

Her heart rate increased. She didn't want to be rude, but dates were out.

"Oh?"

"I spent the afternoon with Mike and an annoying HVAC guy. We have some things we need to go over about what kind of system you want installed. I'd like to get back with him before the weekend, so we can get this thing moving."

Her muscles relaxed with the explanation. "Okay, I'm onboard with that. Was he really annoying?" She caught herself grinning.

"Yeah. You have no idea. I can't wait for you to meet him."

"That's what you're for—to filter the annoying

people out of my life."

"That'll cost you more. You almost done?"

"I am. I'm waiting on some copies."

"Did you find anything interesting?"

"I think so. I really didn't read through everything."

"Hurry up. The pizza's getting cold," he teased.

"Here she comes. I'll be out in a few minutes." She ended the call and was surprised by the warm feeling that passed over her. Brynn looked forward to his company. She pushed away the thought. Being on her own was lonely, and he was someone to talk to. That's all it was.

She gathered her information, thanked the librarian for her help, and headed for the exit. Jax's truck was right outside the door. She climbed in. "Sorry you had to wait." She inhaled the aroma of, what could only be, pepperoni. "That pizza smells delicious."

"You're going to love it." He put the truck in gear and made the short drive back to the Wharf Inn. Jax came around and opened her door with one hand and a pizza in the other.

She blushed at the chivalry and muttered a "thanks" while sliding out. They walked silently back to her room. All kinds of thoughts bounced around her head. *What will people think? Was he getting the wrong idea? Does he consider this a date?*

Brynn unlocked the door and found Romeo waiting, his tail swishing from side to side. She slipped out of her coat and scratched the cat under his chin. He swatted at her hand. "What's got you agitated, Romeo?" It wasn't long before she found the bottle of champagne sitting on the coffee table. She turned to Jax with a questioning look. "Did you…"

"Wasn't me. I think I would have gone with a two liter of Coke this early on in our relationship."

His comment didn't have time to sink in. She grabbed her phone and called the front desk. Romeo could have slipped out. "Hello. This is Brynn Austin from room six. I received a bottle of champagne, and although I appreciate it, I'm concerned my cat could have escaped."

"Mrs. Austin, we didn't send any champagne to your room."

"What? Then, who?" The blood drained from her face, and she turned to find Jax beside her. "How would someone have gotten into my room?"

"I'm not sure, and it's definitely a concern. Would you like us to notify the police?"

She stopped to think. What was she going to say? *Someone left me a bottle of champagne. I want them arrested.* They found people who took things. "No…no. But if you see anyone entering my room, please stop them. I'm staying here by myself."

"I'll be sure to report this to the owner. I'm sorry."

"It's not your fault." She hung up and lowered herself to the couch. The wheels in her head turned.

"What are you thinking?" Jax asked.

"That I'm a paranoid cop's wife. Does it look like it's been tampered with?" Brynn watched while Jax looked it over.

"No. The foil's intact." He returned it to the coffee table.

"So, do you want champagne with that pizza?" She needed to relax.

"Sure. Why not? It might make the HVAC guy

look better."

Brynn laughed at the comment and excused herself to search for a corkscrew. She found one in the community room. "Would you mind doing the honors? I can't handle the suspense."

The cork flew across the room, and Brynn shrieked at the noise. She handed him two foam cups. "Only the best crystal for our…" She stopped herself.

"You were going to say date, weren't you?"

Brynn bit down on her lip, and tears filled her eyes. She didn't trust herself to speak, only nodded in answer.

Jax sat next to her on the couch and took her hand in his. "It's okay, Brynn. There's no need to be embarrassed. I'd take you on a date in a heartbeat if I thought you were ready. You're not. Let's just drink some of this, and relax, okay? Just two friends eating pizza?"

She eased her hand out of his. "I'm not sure if I'll ever be ready for more with anyone…ever. Nate was the love of my life. The thought of dating someone else…it would be such a betrayal to what we had."

"When you're ready to move on, you'll know it."

He had been so nice to her, and all she kept talking about was how she didn't want to date him. Did she hurt his feelings? "I'm not saying you're not attractive," she blurted, regretting it immediately.

"I'm attracted to you too, Brynn. You're a beautiful woman."

"Oh, God. I can't believe I just said that out loud." Her stomach churned at the admission. She covered her face with her hands. She was beyond embarrassed. Horrified would be more like it. Why couldn't she just eat the pizza and shut her mouth?

Jax pulled her hands away, and held them in his. "Losing your husband, and in such a tragic way, has to be unbearable. Don't beat yourself up. You're going to have these feelings about other men. I'd say it's probably even normal." He paused with a smile, and tilted his head. "I'd like to think I'm special and ahead of the curve, but…"

"Maybe it's best we don't see each other, other than castle business."

"Is that what you want?" he asked in a low voice.

"I wish I could rewind the conversation before I stuck my foot in my mouth. Then, we could go back to being friends, and all this wouldn't seem so awkward."

"We can do that. We'll get this castle done and have some fun in the meantime. No strings. Just a couple of besties."

Brynn smiled at the word *besties,* but it quickly faded. If only it could be that easy…

Chapter Seven

Brynn sorted the information by subject; articles with pictures of the interior, information about Sebastian Morgan's business, his wife, the building of the castle, and his rivalry with his business partner. "Look, Jax. Here's a story about his wife's disappearance."

"What does it say?"

She perused the article, gleaning the highlights. "It looks like the same information." She read further. "Wait a minute. It says Helena told a friend if anything happened to her, she was murdered."

"Does it say if anyone was accused?" Jax lowered himself next to her with another piece of pizza.

"No. Not really. It only says her husband was being held for questioning, and the police were investigating." She placed the article in the proper stack. "Do you think he did it?"

"Sebastian?"

She nodded. "It seems plausible. I'm sure domestic violence isn't something that started in this century. And maybe that's why the castle has sat empty for so many years. According to all the information I can gather, Sebastian and Helena were the only people to live in the castle for longer than two years."

"What are you saying? The ghosts of Sebastian and Helena walk the halls?" He held up the champagne bottle. "More?"

Brynn lifted her glass. "Not too much." She continued her hypothesis. "Not real ghosts, but negative energy."

"Okay, now you're losing me."

"People hear the stories, and imaginations run wild." She sipped from her cup. "Why would it sit empty for so long?"

"My guess? People underestimate the cost of maintaining a place that large."

She shifted on the couch, facing him. "Do you think I'll be another casualty?" Somehow it mattered what he thought.

"I think you'll have a good chance of making a go of it. You have a viable business plan. Those other people thought they could live there. It had to have been a money pit."

"Yeah, maybe. I sure hope so. This is very important to me."

His eyes connected with hers. "I know it is. I told you before, I'm going to do my best to help you make this happen."

Brynn leaned in and kissed him on the cheek. "That means a lot to me, Jax. Thanks." To her surprise she wasn't embarrassed by the show of emotion. Maybe it was the champagne. But, one thing was for sure, for the first time since Nate's death she wasn't alone.

The wide-eyed look on Jax's face gave her pause. "I'm sorry. I didn't mean to be…what I mean to say is…did I offend you? That was a little forward of me."

"No, Brynn. I'm not offended. More in the neighborhood of stunned."

Heat spread through her body, starting with her

face. Definitely the champagne. "I guess the bubbles are getting to me. I shouldn't have kissed you. It wasn't a romantic kiss, but a thank you kiss," she bumbled on. "It's nice not to feel alone."

"You're not alone, Brynn. Not as long as I'm around." He stood abruptly. "I have to get going. Early day tomorrow working on a castle."

She followed him to the door. "I'd like to stop by and take a look around the lower level. I want my private quarters to be on the main floor."

"I'll be there around eight. We'll have the place heated up."

"You never told me about the HVAC guy. Does he have the furnace installed already?"

"No. We have heaters for construction sites. We were supposed to pick out a system tonight."

"Oh. We got off track, didn't we?"

"It's okay. I kinda like the track we were on. We'll talk about it tomorrow." He stared at her a moment and leaned in and pecked her on the cheek. I had a nice time tonight. It's been awhile since I did anything, but work."

Brynn attempted to control her breathing. She had to admit she enjoyed the evening too. Now, if she could quit analyzing every move he made. He understood they were friends. And he was a good-looking guy…okay, gorgeous, so it was natural her heart was thumping out of her chest.

Brynn thanked him for the pizza and closed the door behind him. Romeo stretched in front of her, having kept a low profile while Jax was there. Brynn walked over to the window to pull the blind. Her eye caught a man in the shadows, staring in the direction of her window. Goosebumps traveled up her arms. She quickly lowered the blind. Her pulse quickened. She shut off the light and peeked out the window. He was gone. Maybe he was out walking and curious about the inside of this old inn. Yes. That had to be it. All this talk about Sebastian and Helena Morgan had her brain conjuring up all kinds of weird things. She breathed a sigh of relief at her dramatics.

Her cell rang next to her. She eyed the clock—nine p.m. The caller ID read Paul Wainright. He was the last person she expected to hear from. She inhaled a shaky breath before answering. "Hello."

"Hi, Brynn. It's Paul Wainright, NYPD. I hope I haven't caught you at a bad time."

"Hi, Paul. You're fine. What can I do for you?" She attempted to portray a calm she wasn't feeling. There was only one reason he'd be calling, and it wasn't to see how she was doing.

"We might have a lead to prove Apollo Bank's involvement in Nate's murder."

The mention of Nate's killer sickened her. "How? It's been over a year."

"Word on the street is Nate had some evidence against the ring that could put Apollo and his right hand man behind bars for a good, long time. We've been through the evidence room with a fine toothed comb, and came up short. Do you have any boxes that might have had some of Nate's stuff from his locker? Or something maybe you haven't gone through yet?"

Brynn would not have them rifling through his things. She couldn't. Not yet. Besides, those boxes were in storage in New York. "No, Paul. I'm sorry. There's nothing here that I haven't been through."

"Would you mind if we drove out and took a look? Maybe it's something you wouldn't think would be evidence."

For some reason, the request put her on guard. He was trying to nail Apollo. Why was she getting that *hair standing up on the back of her neck* feeling? She could hear Nate. *Trust your gut.*

"I'm sorry. I don't have everything out of storage yet. I'm staying in a temporary location. As soon as I get settled I'll give you a call."

"The sooner, the better, Brynn. We want to nail these guys."

"I understand. I'll be in touch."

"And Brynn?"

"Yes?"

"Watch your back. If they think Nate had something, they might come looking for it. Call us if you have any trouble. You hear?"

Brynn thought about the man outside, but something kept her from sharing.

She hung up the phone with a dread she couldn't shake. She wanted Apollo Banks to pay, didn't she? Why was she dragging her feet? What if they could put his killer behind bars, and she had something that could help?

She had come to Mystic to start a new life…a life Nate wanted to share with her—away from the violence and corruption he dealt with every day. Part of her wanted to forget the phone call and move on. It wouldn't bring Nate back. The inner voice nagged her. She exhaled the breath she'd been holding. For now, she'd push it from her mind. What else could she do? His things weren't here with her, and she had a big day tomorrow planning her new living quarters. It was time for happier thoughts.

She grabbed some drawing paper and sketched some ideas. Thoughts pushed their way in, no matter how hard she tried to distract herself. She thought back to the day Nate was murdered. Was there anything unusual? All she could remember was him coming home in the middle of the afternoon in plain clothes. He had told her he had stopped to get something he'd forgotten. He was only home a few minutes before kissing her on the top of the head and leaving. That was the last time she saw him alive. Brynn racked her brain. Could he have been dropping something off, not picking something up? She closed her eyes, willing herself to remember. She didn't remember seeing anything in his hands. It was no use.

Brynn's motivation to move into Sebastian's Castle tripled. As soon as she had her own space, the sooner she could send for her things…and Nate's. Maybe there was a clue she overlooked. There was no use dwelling on it now. She redirected the energy into her sketches. She smiled at her work. This was a place she could live happily ever after.

Chapter Eight

Brynn rose from a restless night. She showered, dressed, and downed a bagel before the sun broke the horizon. Romeo yowled in protest when she packed her briefcase with the previous night's drawings. "I'll be back soon, buddy." She patted the top of his head, then slid into her winter coat.

She glanced at the clock. It was seven-thirty. The ride to the castle would take her about ten minutes. The roads were clear, with no fresh layer of snow. Jax, Mike, and their crews wouldn't be there yet. The thought left her skittish. "Oh, what the heck." She grabbed her purse and key, and started for her car. She was being silly.

She rounded the corner, on the top of the hill, and turned onto her property. Her blood pressure increased the closer she got. She silently berated herself. It was time to put on her big girl panties and put all her unfounded, childish, whimsical fears to rest. She would go in there alone.

Then the relief washed over her at the sight of Jax's truck by the entrance, followed by irritation. *She would not depend on him. It was time to depend on Brynn Austin.*

He exited the castle while she parked next to his truck. He smiled and waved in her direction, then lifted a tool box from a compartment on the side of his truck.

Brynn swung open the car door. "Good morning. I thought I'd be the first one here."

"Good morning to you. I woke up early and couldn't get back to sleep. Thought I might as well start the day."

She reached in and grabbed her briefcase. The sun glowed with full force today. She was grateful for the reprieve from the gloomy, overcast skies. Everything looked better by the light of day.

Brynn followed Jax up the steps, trying not to notice the tight fitting jeans and the tool belt hanging at his hips. She was a sucker for a tool belt. Not so long ago, it had been a gun holster. That familiar twist in her gut took hold with the thought. There were the memories and the guilt colliding again. She had to cut herself a break. Jax Maddox was a good looking guy. End of story. No big deal.

"Brynn, did you hear me?"

The mention of her name pulled her from her internal struggle. "I'm sorry, Jax. My thoughts were elsewhere." Thank God he didn't know where.

"I've got the heat going. It should warm up in here fairly quickly. Do you need any help with anything?"

"I'm just going to wander around down here. I did some sketches last night. I was visualizing." She smiled in his direction. "My ideas might not fit the space."

"If we put our heads together I'm sure we can come up with something that would make you happy. Let me know if you need me."

"Thanks. I will." She settled her things on a table in the rotunda. It wasn't long before she pulled off her coat and glanced around the large space. Brynn saw what it could be, or better yet, what it was. The entire reason she and Nate fell in love with this place returned in that moment. The bones of the place were still intact. She looked up into the two-floor rotunda with its huge crystal chandelier hanging from the second floor. Just beyond was the ornate ceiling. Her eyes then traveled to the beautiful marble-carved fireplace that had stood the test of time.

Two long hallways shot off of both sides of the rotunda. The entry hallway had two small rooms to one side. Brynn wasn't sure what their use might have been but was hoping her information from the library might shed some light. She was thinking of using one for an office.

Brynn was aware of voices in the background—probably Mike and his crew. She paid them no mind as she walked across the space, losing herself in another time. The mammoth front room on the north side of the castle was used for a living room. It was located to the right of the front entrance. The builder did nothing on a small scale. A large fireplace was the centerpiece of the far wall. Brynn found it difficult to imagine this had been a homey space. It would be a challenge.

She crossed through the rotunda to another room, on the opposite side of the entrance. It was a smaller room but with an equally impressive fireplace, yet more ornate. Perhaps, it had been a formal drawing room. Brynn slid her hand across the wood mantel and cringed, knowing beautiful woodwork existed under all that white paint.

"Penny for your thoughts."

She glanced at Jax standing in the doorway and forced a smile. "I'm afraid I'm going to need lots of pennies. That ceiling needs replaced."

"I've done a quick inspection, and this room looks the worst. You knew this wasn't going to be easy…or cheap."

"A girl can hope, can't she? And look what they did to this fireplace. I don't understand what goes through some people's minds. Why would they do this?"

"Cheap fix." He shined his flashlight on the subject. "And no sanding involved."

Brynn shook her head. "I'm going to make it beautiful again." She said for her own benefit as much as Jax's.

"I believe you will. Now, are you ready to talk furnaces?"

"Is that HVAC guy here?" She peeked around him.

He laughed. "Not yet, but I expect him sometime today…and we really should have an answer for him."

"Okay. I guess all my decisions can't be about decorating."

"I have the options on the table over here. Let's take a look."

Jax shuffled through blueprints and pamphlets showing her the options. His arm brushed against hers, causing her to lose all thought. She was sure she missed the last few sentences.

"Brynn?"

He really was going to think she was nuts. "Sorry. It's all a bit much to take in." Her voice cracked with emotion.

"What can I do?"

"I'm a wimp, and there's no cure." She swiped at a tear.

"You're not a wimp. This is a lot to take on by

yourself. I think you're brave."

"Or stupid."

"Would you like a suggestion?"

"Please."

He pulled out a blueprint. "This is the system I would go with. It's large enough to handle such a big place without overtaxing itself. It's going to be more efficient in the long run."

"Sold. And Jax?" His eyes met hers. "Thank you."

"It's a suggestion. The decision is yours. And you're welcome." He winked.

"So, when's that heater man coming?" Mike boomed from the doorway. "I need to know his intentions to get this wiring routed in the right direction."

Brynn grinned in Mike's direction. She liked him. He said what was on his mind, and she had a feeling he was another great guy to have on her side. "Keep them in line, Mike."

"I'm trying, little lady, but I'm getting too old for this sh—…stuff. Pardon."

"I'd better calm the electrician. Are you good?" He searched her eyes, and a feeling of calm passed over her.

"I'm good. I'm going to continue my exploration."

"I'm a yell away."

"I appreciate that." She watched him follow Mike into the unknown room.

Brynn turned and headed down the long hallway, opposite of the entrance. A chill filled the air, spreading goosebumps across her skin. The heat definitely hadn't made it to this end of the house.

At the end of the hall was a huge octagon room

with leaded windows placed at eye level around the entire room. Below the windows were wooden cabinets with leaded glass fronts. She noticed a vase in one of the cases and took it out to investigate. She wasn't an antiques dealer so couldn't be sure of the age. She held it to the light and turned it in all directions. The crystal caught the sunshine and sent prisms throughout the room. The beauty mesmerized her. A shuffling noise behind her caught her attention. She turned, expecting to see Jax or Mike, but that's not what she was confronted with. She dropped the vase and screamed.

****

Dear God, that woman had a set of lungs on her. He took advantage of the moment and slipped out the butler's pantry. She was here twenty minutes, and she was already breaking his things. And all these people in his house, with boxes of strange looking tools and a noise that was aching his head. No. This wouldn't do.

He would admit he was curious. The young lady reminded him of his lost love. There was a sadness about her that initially drew him in, but he was over that now. She and her friends were ruining his happy home. But that was about to end.

Chapter Nine

The scream echoed throughout the first floor. Jax dropped his hammer and ran for the last place he remembered seeing Brynn. She stood there, pale as a sheet of paper.

She stared past him. "Brynn, talk to me." He patted her face gently until he saw recognition replace the blank look. "What the hell happened? Did you see a mouse?"

"No. A man was standing right there." She pointed near a door that went to the kitchen area."

Mike yelled to his crew. "I want this place searched from top to bottom." They ran off in different directions. "You okay, little lady? What did he look like?"

Jax waited until she was ready to speak. "You're not going to believe this. In fact, you're probably going to think I've lost my marbles. He was dressed…" She paused. "He dressed like he was from another time."

"He was wearing a costume?" Jax asked.

"No. I don't know. It wasn't from *Costumes are Us.*" Brynn's body shook. She leaned against the wall.

"You don't look good, Brynn. Sit down and put your head between your knees," Jax ordered.

She slid to the floor, adding some deep breaths. She raised her head in Jax's direction. "Do you think he's been living here? Could he be the one who slammed the door the other day?"

"I don't know, honey, but I'm going to find out. Mike, will you stay with her? I want to check around outside."

"Good idea. I won't leave her side."

Jax nodded and was gone.

Brynn lowered her head again. Dear God, had he just called her *honey?*

****

Jax's fists clenched at his sides as he walked the perimeter of the castle. If he found this guy, God help him. The only footprints he found were leading to the work trucks. There was no sign of anyone walking around the rest of the castle. He wasted no time returning to Brynn's side. Whoever it was had to still be in there.

Most of Mike's crew gathered in the rotunda, where Brynn now stood. She was putting up a good front, but he knew she was shaken.

"There's no sign of anyone coming or going. He has to be in here. Let's give it another look around."

"Jax, I'd like to go with you." Brynn's chin went up, and the shoulders went back.

"I don't know…"

"I won't cower in fear. I promise."

"Okay, but you don't leave my side. Understood?" The need to protect her surprised even him. Brynn Austin was fast becoming more than a client.

Jax and Brynn ascended the grand staircase. Brynn brought up a valid point. "What if there are secret passages? It's a castle, after all."

He'd never thought of that. "I suppose anything's possible. Do you remember seeing any blueprints in all the research you did?"

She shook her head. "No, but maybe it's something I need to look into."

"Good idea. For now, we'll check out every room and look for secret buttons." He winked in an attempt to lighten the mood. She looked scared as hell. In a serious tone he said, "I won't let anyone hurt you."

"I know. Are you carrying?" He raised his shirt to reveal his holstered gun. She let out a sigh and a look of determination crossed her face. "Good. Let's do this."

He admired her bravery, but he would have to talk to her about that. He didn't want her to go off looking for some nutcase if no one was with her. And he'd have to broach the conversation in a neutral way. He knew she would balk at any protective feelings he had for her.

They walked silently around the balcony of the rotunda until they reached the rooms that must have belonged to the lady and gentleman of the mansion. The rooms were to the front, facing east, with ample sunlight pouring through the leaded windows. The room was large with parquet flooring that had seen better days. Jax entered a small room off the larger one that might have been a bath or dressing area at one time. Like most of the other rooms, there was a fireplace with intricately carved woodwork. Sebastian Morgan didn't do shortcuts.

Jax slid his hand down both sides of the fireplace. The whole idea of secret passageways sounded out there, but who knew in a place like this? He found nothing.

Brynn followed him into the room next door. It was equal in size with the same layout, only opposite. Nothing unusual here either. They went to the next bedroom and found no one hiding in the dark corners. The last room searched was the library. Jax looked up at the peeling paint. The carved molding was amazing. He'd have to get someone here with a specialty to work on this room.

His thoughts went back to the interloper. There was a door he hadn't noticed before, off the library. A banging noise echoed from the other side, just as he reached for the doorknob. He yanked it open to a small room with spiral steps leading below. He rushed down the steps as quickly as he could. It was a tricky descend. He found himself in a solarium outside the dining room.

Brynn yelled from above. "Do you see anyone?"

He rushed back up the stairs, not wanting to leave her alone. "No. You heard it too, right?" He was beginning to doubt himself.

"Yeah, I heard it. What's going on here?"

He wished he had an answer. Brynn followed him without question back to the main level, down the hall to the dining area. The layout was the same as the second floor. He opened the door to the solarium, and looked up to where they had been minutes before. Wouldn't hurt to take another look.

Mike came around the corner. "Did you find anything?"

"You didn't come upstairs at any time, did you?" Jax asked Mike.

"No. Why? You see something?"

"No, but we heard a banging noise come from a room directly above. I thought maybe someone came down this staircase."

"I didn't see, or hear, anyone. Maybe we should call the police."

"Probably wouldn't hurt." Jax pulled out his cell and dialed. Within ten minutes there were two cruisers sitting outside Sebastian's Castle.

****

He stuck his neck out on this one and let the woman see him. They were getting a little too serious about changes to his house. No one had ever brought workers in. This was spinning out of control. He glanced around his room. Maybe a little fixing up wouldn't be a bad idea. He could scare them out *after* they did some work. A little noise might be tolerable.

Chapter Ten

Jax, Brynn, and Mike were the last ones to leave late that afternoon. The men stood in the rotunda talking about what was on the agenda for the following day.

"Do you think they'll come back?" she blurted.

"Who, little lady?"

"The crew. Or do you think they're going to believe this is haunted and run for the hills?"

Jax answered first. "They'll be back. Listen, Brynn, I don't know what happened here today, and who was wandering around, but maybe it'd be best if you don't come here alone for a while."

She nodded in agreement. After all, she wasn't stupid. "This isn't a problem I expected, that's for sure. It's getting late. I'm going to head home and tackle my stack of papers. Maybe I can find a blue print, or something."

"Sounds like a plan. Brynn…"

"Yes?"

He shook his head. "Nothing. I'll be here at eight tomorrow."

She wondered what was in his head. "Okay. And thanks, to both of you, for all your help."

"Our pleasure. Keep your chin up, little lady. Once whoever it was realizes we aren't going away, they'll move on. Probably a squatter."

She forced a smile. “I hope so. Have a good evening.”

Brynn walked to her car, and once again, got that creepy feeling. She looked up to the same window as she did days before. She knew it to be one of the main bedrooms. She berated herself for even entertaining the thought of ghosts. But who just disappeared into thin air?

Exhaustion set in as soon as she crossed the threshold of her room. She flipped on the light before entering. These short winter days were getting to her…and so was her imagination. Brynn thought back to the champagne bottle and its mysterious appearance. Nate had always taught her to be alert to her surroundings. Maybe someone didn’t like her purchase of the castle and was trying to spook her? She would have to be more careful.

Romeo rubbed against her legs. “You hungry, fella?” It was later than his normal afternoon meal. She filled his bowl and gave him fresh water, then glanced over at the huge pile of papers that awaited her. A hot shower and a cup of tea sounded like a winner. She’d never be able to concentrate as she was right now.

She gathered up some comfortable pajamas and indulged in a longer than usual shower. With the tea made, Romeo laying in front of the fire she had burning, and soft music playing in the background—she was ready to get to work. An hour later, she still hadn’t found what she was looking for. Most of the information was general, or things she already knew. The frustration grew. She thought again about the trunk in the castle attic. Maybe she should let Jax pry it open.

Brynn jumped at the knock on the door. Glancing

at the clock, she wandered who could be here at this hour? The peephole revealed Jax on the other side of the door. What could have brought him here this late? Something had to be wrong. She looked down at her modest pajamas. Everything was covered, but it just seemed a bit too…intimate. *Quit with the overthinking, Brynn!*

She flung the door open. "Jax? Is something wrong?"

"I'm sorry. I probably shouldn't have come."

"Is it the castle? Did you find out something?"

"No, I um…can I come in?"

"Oh, I'm sorry. Yes, come in." She moved to the side and closed the door. "What's going on?"

"I couldn't get you off my mind." He shifted nervously. "I had to make sure you were okay. I wanted to apologize."

"What would you have to apologize for?"

"I'm sorry I didn't find whoever…"

She cut him off. "Listen, Jax, I appreciate all you've done for me, but I'm not your responsibility. I'll be okay. My husband taught me street smarts, self-defense, and paranoia. I got this."

"I know. I know. I keep telling myself the same thing, but I feel protective of you. Can we sit down and talk a minute?"

The nausea rolled through her stomach. Where was he going with this? "Sure. Have a seat."

The dim lighting coupled with the soft glow of the fire, and the snow falling outside her window screamed romance. Well, she couldn't douse the fire, but she could get rid of the music. Her mind raced to what she would say to any advances.

"I had a couple ideas I wanted to run past you."

"Ideas?" This wasn't where she imagined this late evening conversation would go. She had to admit, relief washed over her.

"Yeah. I know my job is to do the grunt work, and make sure what I can't do, someone else does, but…" Jax hesitated.

"Go on. If you have some suggestions, I'd like to hear them. You've been around this business for a long time. Your input would be appreciated." She thought of her husband.

"It has more to do with the carriage house, than the castle itself."

He had her attention. The two-story carriage house, a short distance from the mansion, was converted to a garage years ago, but was badly in need of repairs, or so Nate had told her. At the time, she wasn't interested in an old dirty garage. "Go on."

"I'm not sure if it's in your budget, but I was thinking it would be great for additional rooms. It would bring in more income, and you could decorate it to fit its prior use—more of a rustic appeal, than the castle."

It might stretch the budget, but it was a great idea. "I like it. I would have to send the idea to my architect, and we'd have to submit the plans," she thought aloud.

"I could do the plans for you," he offered. "And I wouldn't charge you."

"Oh, Jax, I couldn't allow you to do it for free."

"I'd actually enjoy it. I haven't utilized my architectural degree in a long while."

"I had no idea. When did you find time to do that?"

"I never slept."

Brynn laughed. "If you take this on, you're going to lose some more."

"It will give me something else to focus on when I'm pacing the floors at two a.m."

"It's tough when something's on your mind you can't shake." Her last year had involved little sleep.

"Not something, someone," he muttered. "Well, I should be going. Sorry for dropping by on you."

Brynn couldn't explain it, but she didn't want him to leave. She hadn't missed his comment about getting someone off his mind. He looked torn. She knew that feeling. Brynn was having it now. She wanted Jax to stay and yet guilt washed over her when thoughts of Nate crept in. Maybe she could offer Jax friendship, and ease him through the breakup he must be going through. Sometimes it helped just to talk about it.

"Would you like to stay for tea?" she offered.

"Tea?" He smiled.

"Yes. Tea. I don't have anything else. I need to find a grocery store, so I can stock that tiny, little refrigerator." She was babbling.

"I'd love to."

"It's not brewed. I only have a microwave."

"It's the company, not the tea, Brynn."

Her face warmed at the comment. "I'll just be a few minutes." She concentrated at the task at hand and took a deep breath before bringing him his cup.

"Thanks."

She sat down on the opposite side of the couch. The blinds were still open, and by the lamplight she could see the snow falling heavily. There was a low light on in the corner, and fire crackling in front of them. Brynn glanced over at him. He stared into the fire and sipped his tea. Jax Maddox was an incredibly handsome man. His light brown hair was cut short. It suited him. He emanated strength, and it wasn't just from the obvious muscles. Maybe that was why she was drawn to him. She lacked that in her life.

"Do you want to talk about it?" she asked. The silence was getting a bit awkward.

He sat his tea on the table in front of them. "Talk about what?"

"The woman you're trying to get over. Maybe I can help."

He chuckled.

"Sometimes talking about it helps."

"I don't think that applies here." He shook his head, and a grin spread across his face.

"What? You don't think I'm a good listener?" She tried not to be offended. "I know we've only known each other a few weeks, but I think we've become friends."

His grin disappeared. "Are you sure you want to hear what's on my mind?"

Now she wasn't so sure…

Chapter Eleven

"If you don't want to talk about it, I'm not going to force you."

Jax shifted. "I have feelings for someone, and I'm not sure what to do about it."

The tension in Brynn's body was gone with that one sentence. She'd been over-analyzing their friendship. He wanted her advice. This was good. "Okay. You haven't told her?"

"No, not really. I don't want to ruin a good thing."

Brynn nodded. She understood that. "I met Nate through a mutual friend. We would all hang out. He was like another buddy, until one day I really looked at him. I realized this was the kind of guy I wanted to spend the rest of my life with."

"How did you get past the buddy thing?"

"Honestly, I decided one day to hang my neck over the chopping block. Eight months later we were married." She smiled fondly at the memory. "Tell her how you feel. What's the worst that could happen?"

"I could get fired." He smirked at his own joke.

"How in the world do you have time to work at another…?" She stopped mid-sentence, and it dawned on her. "Jax?"

"Yeah, Brynn, it's you."

Her stomach pitched.

"My neck's on the chopping block. What are you

going to do?" There was fear in his eyes.

"Wow. I'm speechless." A nervous laugh escaped. "I'm never speechless." She ran her hands through her curly, blonde hair. "I'm flattered."

"That's what a guy wants to hear. You don't have to say anything. I know you're going through stuff, and I'd probably never live up to the type of man your husband was, but…"

"Jax, that's definitely not what I was thinking. I'm still mourning him, yes, but I think you're a wonderful person. I like being around you." She saw the skepticism in his face. "I do. Really. I've never thought of moving on."

"And what if you did? What would you think about dating me?"

Honesty. There had to be honesty between them. "We're working together. I need you. What if it went bad? I'd be looking for a new contractor." There wasn't anything wrong with a little humor.

"And what if it went right? You'd get me at a reduced rate."

The corners of her mouth turned up with a small smile. He had a way of making the most awkward situation bearable. Brynn definitely liked him and enjoyed his company. Tonight she hadn't wanted him to leave.

"I'm sorry. I should have stuck with the sleepless nights."

"No, Jax. It's okay. I'm glad you told me. I'm not sure how to handle it, that's all."

"Well, that can't be good." He stood and looked out the window. "I'd better head out. The snow's really coming down."

"Don't run away from this," she said softly, standing behind him.

He turned and faced her. They were inches apart. "I'm not running. I'm trying to give you an out."

"I haven't had a chance to tell you what's on my mind." She folded her arms in front of her, looking down, willing the right words to come out of her mouth. How did she make him understand? Her instinct was to look anywhere, but in his eyes. She feared what she would find, but she had to. She had to let him see what was in her heart. "Nate's gone. Every day I wake up from the same nightmare. My husband was murdered, and he's never coming back. How does a person move on from that?"

"I don't know, Brynn. I should go." He reached for his coat on the chair.

"No, you shouldn't. We have to talk through this now. It will hang between us. Sit," she ordered. "My focus is making this dream we had come true. I never figured someone like you into the equation." Words were pouring out, and honestly, she didn't know what was going to come out of her mouth. He remained silent. "I really like you, Jax. Tonight, when you were going to leave, I didn't want you to go." She hurried on. "It's not like…"

"Like what?"

"You know…sexual. You're very attractive. Oh God, I didn't want to go there. How did I end up there?" Her hands went to her face.

"Well, it's nice to know I'm not an ogre."

Her teeth were going to go through her lip if she bit down any harder. She backpedaled. "I didn't expect someone who would care about me, or what I was trying to accomplish. I appreciate that."

"I'm not going for appreciation, sunshine," he said in a low tone.

There was that word again. Why did it make her mind go to putty? "Can we spend time together without strings? I like being with you. I love your input. I love that someone else cares about this castle, but romance? I can't make that move right now. I think, if that happens, it won't be something I consciously decide."

"So, you're not ruling it out?"

Brynn didn't want to give him false hope. "I can't make promises, but no, I'm not ruling it out."

"Would you be opposed to time spent beyond the renovation?"

"Like?"

"I feel like I'm in negotiations." He attempted humor again. She liked that about him. "Dinner now and then, maybe a movie, a walk along the water…just stuff that doesn't have to do with blueprints. I want you to know me. There's more to me than a tool belt."

Actually, she was fond of the tool belt, but right now wasn't the time to bring that up. "I'm not opposed, as long as we keep it friendly."

"I'll let you lead."

She nodded. "I can live with that."

"It's a deal, then. Should I have the contract sent to you?" He shoved an arm into his coat.

"I don't think we need this one in writing. We could shake on it" She reached out her hand.

Jax slowly raised her hand to his lips, never taking his eyes from hers. "Goodnight, Brynn. I think, tonight, I'll be able to sleep."

She wasn't so sure she would.

****

Jax left Brynn's place with hope. It was a long time, since a woman had turned his head for anything less than a casual affair. He was too busy for relationships. Leave it to him to pick someone with baggage. He believed her heart would heal, and he would be the one to help her through it.

He stopped and looked into the night sky. "Nate Austin, if you're listening, let me make her happy again. I promise to keep her safe." Maybe it was stupid, but if there was a chance he was listening, he needed all the help he could get.

Chapter Twelve

Brynn rose to a new day with a cloud of doubt and a tad of nervousness hanging over her head. She prayed things with Jax wouldn't be awkward. She'd have to make sure that didn't happen. She needed him. Needed his expertise, or this bed and breakfast would never happen. She threw on some old clothes, grabbed a cup of coffee, scratched Romeo under the chin, and headed into the unknown. Not far from her mind was yesterday's visitor—and the mace Nate had bought her, tucked into her sweatshirt pocket.

She expected to see Jax's truck already there, but Mike's vehicle was the only one by the entrance. Disappointment washed over her. He was mad, or the very least, avoiding her. She let out a nervous breath, wondering what Jax told Mike about his absence.

"Hey Mike," she yelled. "It's Brynn."

"Back here, little lady." She smiled at his nickname for her and followed the sound of his voice. He was in the dining area where she had been visited last night.

"Good morning, Mike. You're busy already."

"Just a few more things to do, and you'll have electric on the first floor."

Excitement bubbled up. "Really? You know what that means? I can move in here soon."

"Are you sure you want to do that? You know, with what happened here yesterday?" He looked down at her from the top of the ladder, peering over his glasses.

Brynn was touched by his concern. "I'm sure. How about I put you on speed dial?"

"That would be a start, but you'd better add Jax to that list. He worries about you like an old mother."

The comment reminded her of the conversation they had last night. "Where is Jax?"

"He had to make a run to the hardware store. He should be back any minute."

Well, at least, it wasn't that he was mad at her. "Okay, Mike, I've got a few things on my list. Yell if you need me."

"Likewise, little lady, likewise."

The first thing on her list was the attic. She wanted another look at that trunk. It was locked for a reason, and she wanted to know why. She grabbed a screwdriver from the table in the rotunda and headed for the second floor. Her heart pounded a little harder with each step, but she refused to allow her imagination to get the best of her. This was *her* home now.

She reached the attic door and climbed with purpose, not as a victim, but a person with confidence. Something Nate had taught her. Never show weakness. If you walked like a victim, your mind would believe it…along with everyone else.

Light shone in through the windows, but the space wasn't any less creepy. Old cobwebs hung from the rafters, and dust particles danced in the sunlight. She hoped there wasn't a family of raccoons, or worse, living here. Brynn pushed those thoughts from her mind and kneeled in front of the trunk with the screwdriver. She'd never tried to pick a lock before, but there was a first time for everything.

"If you're set on nosing around, I would rather you used the key. It's under that pile of books."

Brynn jumped to her feet and swung around to face the voice. She gripped tightly to her only weapon, the screwdriver.

There he stood, the same man she saw the other day. "Who are you?" She backed toward the wall, holding the screwdriver in front of her. "You're trespassing."

"No, my dear, you're trespassing. This is my castle. I should be asking you the questions."

Brynn's eyes bugged out as she *really* took a look at him. His image was fading in and out. "No," she said aloud, "it can't be."

"My dear, you don't look well."

"You're a…" She patted her face.

"A what? I'm a what?" His face faded and returned.

"You're a ghost!" Brynn sat on the trunk. The room spun in every direction.

"That's preposterous! My name is Sebastian Morgan, and I'm the owner of this castle."

She rubbed her hands up and down her arms. No, she wasn't dreaming this. "Sebastian Morgan died in 1934. It's 2016."

"That's poppycock," he harrumphed. "I am a flesh and blood human being." He pinched himself. And again. "This is not possible."

"I saw you. Yesterday, in the dining room."

"I attempted to scare you off. Apparently, I failed." He held his arms in front of him, studying them. His head raised. The look of doubt was quickly replaced with an authoritative voice. "You cannot stay. This is my home, and it's becoming quite noisy since your arrival."

"It belongs to me." Was she really arguing with a ghost? No. There had to be an explanation. An elaborate hoax? She glanced toward the steps. Should she scream?

"It seems we have come to an impasse. I cannot allow you to stay." He raised his chin stubbornly. "And may I ask, why you're rooting around my attic?"

"I'm looking for blueprints of the mansion. I thought if I could find the secret passages that must exist, I could find the person who's been sneaking around here."

"Who's sneaking around?" He cocked his head.

"You?"

"Me? Why in the devil would I sneak around my own home?" The more worked up he became, the more his image faded in and out.

"How do I put this?" Brynn's fear subsided. Real or imagined, it didn't appear he intended to hurt her. The only fear now was the distinct possibility she'd lost her mind.

"I'm waiting."

An impatient ghost…great.

"You're not alive."

"How do you explain my existence?"

He had her there. "I can't. Up until a few minutes ago, I didn't believe in ghosts." But, boy, this did explain some things.

"Well, at any rate, you and your friends will have to leave." He stood tall and tugged on the lapel of his suit, making adjustments to something that didn't exist.

Or did it?

Irritation boiled up and replaced shock. "I'm not going anywhere." She'd invested too much into this place to be ruined by some poltergeist who wouldn't follow the light.

"We shall see about that. I will drag out my chains and scare your help away."

"I thought you weren't a ghost?" She pushed back.

"I am not, but it worked previously to remove unwanted visitors from my domain."

"You'd better take another look. You might change your mind."

Sebastian held his arms in front of him, and his eyes widened at what he saw. His hands had disappeared. "I don't believe it. It can't be."

Brynn couldn't help feeling a bit sorry for him. She watched him evaporate into the daylight, leaving her all alone to process what happened.

****

"Brynn?" Jax called to her from the bottom of the attic stairs.

She closed her eyes and sucked in two big breaths before answering. "Up here."

"What are you doing? You should have told someone where you were. We don't know who's wandering around here."

She did. "Yeah, you're right. I'm sorry." She held up the screwdriver. "I was going to pick the lock."

He reached out his hand for the tool. "You want some help?"

"Actually, I think I know where the key is." She walked over to the stack of books and lifted. Underneath the bottom book was a key, just like

Sebastian said. Brynn held it up with satisfaction.

"How did you know that was there?" A deep line of confusion ran between his eyebrows.

"Sebastian's ghost told me." Might as well stay close to the truth.

"Sure, Brynn. Seriously, how did you find it?"

Okay, she'd go with the second explanation. "I was poking around and found it under the books. I'm a sucker for a good book."

"So, why haven't you opened it already?"

"I was a little nervous. With all the stories circulating, visions of a dead body crammed inside slowed me down."

"Hand over the key."

And honestly? She was nervous about what was inside. Sebastian hadn't given her a clue. Helena Morgan was never found, so anything was possible.

Jax kneeled in front of the trunk. "You ready?" he asked, looking over his shoulder to where she stood.

She nodded, not trusting words.

He turned the key, lifting the lid carefully. The creaking noise added to an already eerie moment. His head blocked the view, and she was okay with that. She needed a minute to gather some courage. She peered over his shoulder and gasped.

Chapter Thirteen

All thoughts of blue prints left her mind when her eyes landed on a stunning gold silk gown, covered in lace. “Jax, it’s beautiful.” She kneeled next to him and ran her hand over the material.

“It is that.” He smiled at her and snickered. “You’re all female, aren’t you?”

“What’s that supposed to mean?”

“You see a shiny piece of clothing, and you forget your mission.”

“Touché.” She gently lifted the dress and held it up in front of her. The detail took her breath away. Brynn glanced over at Jax, expecting some snide comment, but what she caught was him staring at her with a look she wished she’d never seen…admiration.

“You missed your century. No one would have touched your beauty.”

Brynn folded the dress over her arm, and laid it carefully on the red velvet couch. She cleared her throat. “Anything else in there?”

Jax pulled out a wooden box and flipped open the lid. Pictures. About fifty of them. Brynn truly had found a treasure chest. There were old gloves, a couple of hats, scarves, nothing that would shake her world, until…he pulled out a leather-bound book, opened it, and she saw the eloquent hand-writing of a woman. Could it be?

"Is it Helena's?"

Before Jax could answer, she saw movement in the corner of the room. There, once again, stood Sebastian with a look of sorrow that belonged in a funeral home. Brynn sucked in her bottom lip, hoping he would fade out before Jax saw him. She didn't want to lose her general contractor. Word would get out about Sebastian the ghost, and she'd never get this completed.

"Brynn, what are you looking at?"

There was no way to stop him before he looked in the direction of Sebastian Morgan. She held her breath.

"Did you hear me? Are you okay?"

Jax didn't see him? Sebastian was standing there plain as day. "I'm fine. Daydreaming." She took the journal from his hands and opened to the first page. It simply read, *The days and nights of Helena Baldridge Morgan ~ 1901*

Her hands shook with excitement. "There might be a clue in here to how she died."

Jax stood and peered over her shoulder. "Who knows, this might have the answers to an unsolved mystery. What do you want me to do with the other stuff?"

Brynn glanced casually to the corner where she saw Sebastian. He was gone. Her heart sank just a bit. He had looked so sad, but at what?

"Brynn? The stuff?"

"You can put it back in the trunk but leave the pictures out."

"And the dress?"

"It's gorgeous, but I don't think I could wear it to the grocery store."

"How about on a first date?"

She groaned. "I thought we were past that conversation."

"We are…for now." Jax packed the things back into the trunk. "I'm heading back down and maybe get some work done. You're one hell of a distraction."

Brynn ignored the comment and flipped through the pages, looking for something to jump out at her, but nothing did.

"Are you coming?" he asked.

"In a few." He didn't move. "I'll scream really loud if I see anyone."

A suspicious glance flew in her direction, but he nodded and disappeared down the steps.

"Can I see that?"

Brynn spun around. Sebastian was standing behind her. It belonged to his wife. It was only right to hand it over.

He took it gingerly in his hands and held the book to his face, closing his eyes. Turning to the first page, she watched his attention settle on Helena's handwriting. "It would not be appropriate for me to read her thoughts." He closed the book and handed it back to Brynn.

Guilt washed over her. "If you don't want me to read it, I won't. We'll put it back in the trunk and lock it up."

"That would be hard to explain to your beau."

"He's not my beau. He's my contractor." Why did she need to explain herself to a ghost?

"I saw the way his eyes watched your every move. He's smitten."

"He's not."

"He is."

"Would you please stop arguing with me, Casper?"

"Who is Casper?"

"Never mind. I need to get downstairs, or they'll come looking for me. They think someone is living in this house."

"Someone is…me. And I've no intention of leaving my home."

"We're going to have to come to some kind of understanding, because I spent a lot of money buying this place, and I'm not leaving either." She stood with her shoulders back and spoke with confidence, just like Nate had taught her.

"You can stay as my guest," he conceded.

"Will you promise not to scare the workers?"

His nose wrinkled as if he'd whiffed a can of sardines. "I cannot make promises. They're demolishing my home."

"Have you looked around, Mr. Morgan? It's not in the best shape. I'm trying to change that." He lifted his chin. Brynn wasn't sure if it was in protest, or if she made some headway. "What if I pass everything by you first?"

"What do you mean by pass?"

She had his attention. "Consult with you on the renovations. I want this castle to be beautiful again."

He nodded curtly. "I would like that too. Helena did all the decorating."

"I found pictures of how it looked in its glory. What if I tried to capture that again? Would you be agreeable?"

"Brynn? Who are you talking to up there?" Jax yelled up.

Brynn whispered to Sebastian, "We'll talk about

our plans later."

He bowed in her direction and disappeared. "I'm coming." Would Jax believe she was reading aloud? Brynn stepped down the first step and looked over her shoulder, and smiled. She was in cahoots with a ghost. How cool was that?

Chapter Fourteen

Brynn rounded the corner and spotted Jax with a worker she wasn't acquainted. Tall and lanky, with salt and pepper hair, it appeared the unknown man was doing most of the talking.

"Brynn, I'd like you to meet the HVAC man, Fred Simms."

The grin on Jax's face was difficult to ignore. A face to face meet with the annoying HVAC guy—just what she needed. "Nice to meet you, Fred."

"It's a pleasure to meet you, Mrs. Austin. A real pleasure I say. We've been working hard to get this heat on for you. Yes, sir. Putting in some long hours. Should be ready to flip the switch late this afternoon, or early morning. I'll bet you'll be glad to have some heat moving around here. Yes, sir. It's real cold this time of year."

Sebastian appeared directly behind Fred with an eyebrow raised.

Brynn's head was spinning. And it didn't help she was waiting for Jax to see Sebastian. Her nerves were on overload. "Thank you, Fred, for your hard work. I'm looking forward to the warmth."

"It wasn't the hardest job I've ever done, mind you, but it was a humdinger. There's a lot of square footage to cover, and…"

"Does he come up for air?" Sebastian's snide

comment horrified Brynn. She was sure someone had to have heard it. When neither Jax, nor Fred, made notice of it, she realized she still had a chance to get Sebastian out of the room before he became visible to others.

She swatted the air, hoping Sebastian got the hint to leave. He shrugged his shoulders and evaporated.

"Brynn, what are you doing?" Jax's puzzled look had her panicking for a logical explanation to her animated behavior.

"There was a fly. Didn't you see it?"

"In the middle of winter?" He obviously wasn't convinced.

A quick exit would be for the best. "If you'll both excuse me, I have something I need to take care of before I leave for the day." A conversation with Sebastian about the proper behavior expected of a ghost was high on the list.

"Did you need help?" Jax asked.

The meaning behind the raised eyebrows and forced smile on Jax's face wasn't lost on Brynn. She didn't need Fred following her around. No, he'd have to take one for the team.

She smiled back at him. "You two finish up your conversation. I'll be fine." She expected Jax would get even, but for now, she had a ghost to track down.

Brynn grabbed her briefcase from the dining room, where she'd left it, and climbed the attic steps one more time. Sebastian was nowhere to be found. The journal sat on top of the trunk. Should she? He hadn't said he didn't want her to read it.

"Sebastian?" she called, barely above a whisper. Nothing. She glanced around the attic. She picked up the journal gingerly, before placing it in her bag. She shoved her arms into her coat, grabbed her purse and made a run for it—past Jax, and the HVAC man. No way was she getting stuck in the middle of that conversation.

The decision was made quickly, once she got safely in her car, to stop by the pub for some dinner. A cheeseburger sounded delicious. She needed to think, and sitting alone in her room didn't appeal to her, even if Romeo was a good listener.

A thought occurred. What if Sebastian followed her home? No…could he? She didn't know the rules. *Really, Brynn, you're sounding like an insane person.*

"Good afternoon, Mrs. Austin." He glanced up to the clock over the bar. "Or should I say evening? All alone tonight?"

"I am, Charlie. I'm starved. Can you fry me up one of those amazing cheeseburgers?"

"I'd be happy to. For here, or to go?"

"I'll eat here." She shook out of her coat. She spent too much time in her room. The only person she really saw was Jax. And Mike, on and off. Maybe seeing so much of one person was making her dependent on him…making her feel things that weren't real. Speaking of real—Sebastian Morgan's ghost. She shook her head. She had to have imagined all that.

"What can I get you to drink?" Charlie was back after he placed her order. "Beer? Mixed drink?"

"She'll have one of your house beers."

The voice belonged to Jax Maddox. She'd know it anywhere. Turning, she squinted at him. "I will? Maybe I wanted a cup of coffee." He pulled out the barstool and sat next to her. "Sure, have a seat."

"You weren't going to ask me to join you?" He

feigned a hurt expression.

"We spend too much time together. People are going to get ideas. Besides, I need to learn to depend on myself." She pretended to watch the basketball game on the big screen.

"Hey, I saw you alone and thought maybe you'd like some company. I can move."

Brynn let out a breath full of guilt. "I'm sorry. You're fine. I shouldn't care so much what people think. As long as we both know this is just a friendly dinner."

"Tell them whatever you want. We're talking business, we're discussing zoning, or you could tell them you're trying to desensitize yourself to my good looks."

She fired off a warning glance. Although, he wasn't far off the mark. "Watch that high opinion of yourself."

Charlie placed a beer in front of them both. "Thanks, man." Jax took a drink, then asked, "So, did you have time to look over that journal at all?"

"Not really." She thought back to what Sebastian had said, and apprehension replaced excitement. "I almost feel like I'm intruding."

"She's long gone. And what if there's something in there that would explain her disappearance and clear Sebastian Morgan's name?"

"Do you think that's relevant now?" Brynn sipped her beer.

"It's an open case here, I'm sure. And think of the publicity it could bring your bed and breakfast."

"I suppose." Her mind wandered again to Sebastian and the forlorn look on his face when she found the diary.

"You don't seem too excited. It's better than a dead body."

She nearly choked on her beer.

"All right. What's going on?"

"I don't know. Finding the journal started me thinking. Do I have a right to poke into someone else's business? It was hidden away in a locked trunk." She turned to him. "What would you do?"

"Read it. They had no kids. There's no family here. You wouldn't be hurting anyone, no matter what you found out."

"Wouldn't I? Maybe I'd be tarnishing their memories." She hadn't realized how torn she was over this until she started talking to Jax.

"Maybe you'll be clearing a name."

"Sebastian?"

"Yeah. According to the locals, a cloud has hung over him since her disappearance. If you find out she ran off with his rival, his name is cleared."

"Or I'd humiliate him." Charlie slid the cheeseburger on the bar in front of her.

"Thanks." She smiled in his direction, while her stomach grumbled an approval.

"He's no longer here to be humiliated." Jax bit into his cheeseburger.

Yeah, that's what you think... She needed the subject changed. "So, did you guys get the heat turned on?"

"No, I made a judgment call. I thought it'd be best to wait until morning. I'll be there all day if there're any problems."

"Are you thinking inferno?" Her nerves heightened

at the thought.

"I'm sure everything's fine. I'd rather be careful."

"Agreed. When do you think I can move in?"

"How finished do you want it?" His reply was said with humor, but she knew there was truth to the comment.

Brynn had chosen the old servants' quarters near the kitchen to remodel for her space. There were three modest sized rooms. A wall had already been removed to create a nice living area.

"I just need a place to throw a bed, a table, and a chair. It doesn't have to be in my quarters."

"I'm in the process of sanding paint off of wood molding. Why the hell anyone would do that is beyond me. You pick out a paint color, and I should be able to paint soon. I'd also like to get the two fireplaces checked if you intend on using them."

"I'd like to. Thanks. I hadn't thought of that."

"Maybe by next weekend? And that's extremely optimistic even if I spend every waking moment there."

They finished their meals with no more talk of the castle, journals, or romance. Jax focused on the game playing on TV, and let out the occasional complaint. Brynn was reminded of evenings like this with Nate. He was always the armchair quarterback. She didn't know much about sports but always enjoyed watching with him. Her eyes welled with unshed tears. Jax didn't notice, and she was grateful she wouldn't have to explain.

After dinner, and a break in the basketball action, Jax walked her to her car. Brynn feared he was going to try to kiss her, but he didn't—wishing her only a good evening.

Back at her room, she settled on the couch with Romeo in her lap. She held the journal in her hands, examining the leather cover. The smell of perfume drifted to her nose. She wondered what kind of person Mrs. Helena Morgan was. Did she run off with Sebastian Morgan's nemesis, or did something sinister happen? Maybe she'd read just one entry before turning in…

Chapter Fifteen

Brynn read.

We have called the castle home now for six months. I walk the halls and still find it difficult to believe I live in a castle, like a princess, I have found my prince. Sebastian has granted me license to decorate as I see fit, and I enjoy the task. It is my greatest joy to see his approval and see his smile when he returns from the shipyard.

One entry turned into four, before she finally turned in for the night. She had written a few notes about references to the decorating, but there wasn't anything too out of the ordinary. Actually, it was boring. One entry was about the weather, and another was about their dinner menu. Brynn hoped the content became a bit more lively, or informative…something.

She brewed her morning cup of coffee and dug in her briefcase for the number to the moving company. One week from today her things would be in the same state with her. Nate's things would be here.

Her thoughts were interrupted by a phone call. A dark cloud hovered over her. It was Detective Wainwright. "Hello."

"Brynn, it's Paul. NYPD. Are you busy?"

"I'm just heading out. What can I do for you?"

"I have some information I want to share with you. It comes from an informant, who's proved reliable in the past."

A chill spread through her with the mention of an informant. Nate had used one while undercover.

"Now, I'm not trying to scare you…"

"Paul, you're having the opposite effect then."

"Apollo Banks is looking for you. Not so much you, but something you might have in your possession. We spoke of this possibility during our last conversation."

Brynn sucked in a breath. "Did your informant say what he intended to do if he found me?"

"From the information we've gathered, we have no reason to believe you're in any danger, but I can't guarantee it. Have you had a chance to look through Nate's things again? Could you have missed something?"

Brynn's alarm bells rang loudly. "No, I'm sorry. I haven't yet."

"Remember to give me a call if you find anything."

"So, what am I supposed to do up here? Just wait for Apollo, or his thugs, to pounce?" The sarcasm came out as she intended. None of this made sense. Shouldn't he be notifying the Mystic Police Department? Or suggesting she did?

"We're watching their every move. If they do anything suspicious, we'll be on them. We aren't going to let anything happen to you, Brynn." He paused. "But it sure would be helpful if we knew what they were looking for."

"Do you think the evidence could prove they murdered Nate?"

"I don't know, at this point. Keep your eyes open."

"Yeah, I will. Keep me posted, okay?" She hung

up with his assurance he would let her know of any developments. She wasn't comforted by that. What if Apollo wasn't the one making the move? What if he hired someone else to do it? They would never see it coming.

Brynn gazed out the window at the river below, and the people walking the wharf. What was so innocent twenty minutes ago had now turned to paranoia. Could any of these people be watching her?

****

The heat was running, and Jax had successfully rid himself of Fred the HVAC guy. Things were looking up. Now, he could concentrate on Brynn's space. He started with sanding paint off of the original woodwork. He muttered a few obscenities. Painting over woodwork like this was plain criminal and should require a jail sentence.

Jax didn't want to rush his way through her rooms, and the weekend deadline wasn't going to happen at any pace, so he'd come up with a plan B. He hadn't run it past her yet, only coming up with it this morning while he showered. If he'd have to guess, she'd be onboard. It would get her in the castle sooner than later.

While he mindlessly sanded, he thought back to their conversation where he admitted his feelings for her. She hadn't said no. God, he thought about her all the time. Had there ever been a time when a woman monopolized his thoughts? He couldn't think of any.

Brynn Austin had beauty, brains, and guts. Most people, man or woman, would have dropped this entire idea going through what she had. But, no, it made her more determined.

With no furniture in the mansion, the sound of the

entrance door latching reverberated throughout the downstairs. "Brynn, that you?" he called.

"It's me," she said from the doorway.

He stopped sanding. Her sun-kissed blonde hair hung in ringlets, and he had to admit, he wanted to kiss the light pink lip gloss off of her lips. *Dammit, Maddox. Friends. You're friends.* He had to redirect his mind. "Are you here to do some sanding?"

He could usually rustle a smile out of her, but not this time. Her face didn't hold the usual expression of excitement when she walked around her castle. "You're upset."

"How could you possibly know that?" Her eyes filled with tears.

Jax dropped the sandpaper on the ground, and walked toward her. "Who made you cry?" He placed a finger under her chin, and forced her eyes to meet his. "I want to know what's going on."

"Jax, I've told you, you're not responsible for my problems."

"No, I'm not. But if I damned well want to help you, no one's going to tell me no. Not even you. Now tell me what's got you so upset."

"A detective from NYPD called me this morning. I shouldn't be getting you involved in this…" Her voice trailed off.

"What did he want, Brynn?" He held back the anger boiling up.

"He called to tell me, more or less, to watch my back. The leader of the gang my husband was investigating apparently believes I'm in possession of something that could implicate him."

"In the murder?"

"He's not sure, but he thinks it's to do with the weapons ring."

"That's it. You're moving in with me."

"No, Jax, I can't."

"And why not? You could be in danger. This isn't about us, Brynn. This is about your safety."

"I appreciate that. I do. But if I show fear, and they're watching, they're going to assume they're right. I'm on alert, and if I see anything suspicious, or one hair stands up on my neck, I'll call the police. I'll be fine."

"I don't like this."

"You don't have to. The one person I answered to is dead." She turned on her heel and left the room. He had crossed that line without meaning to.

Chapter Sixteen

Brynn hadn't meant to be so brash, but she didn't want him to see the fear on her face. These men killed her husband. They meant business, and she wasn't going to put him at risk too. So if he was mad at her, then so be it. She didn't want to drag him into this.

She stood in the rotunda and attempted to control her emotions.

"Brynn?"

She turned to face him but said nothing. She didn't trust her voice not to betray her.

"I'm sorry you think I overstepped my boundaries, but I'm not backing down here. At the very least, we're friends, and friends help each other through a crisis. I think this qualifies. If you won't move in with me, then let me be your bodyguard when you venture out. We'll call someone and get a state of the art security system in here right away. And you'll let me know what's going on. And don't tell me it's not necessary."

"The security system's not a bad idea, but I can't allow you to spend your free time chauffeuring me around. If I act the victim, I'll become one, Jax." The damned water in her eyes threatened to overflow.

"I can pretend I don't care about you, but we both know it's a lie."

"I appreciate your concern."

"Brynn, stop it. I don't give a shit what people

think. Your husband would want me to do this."

Now, she was angry. "That's not fair. You don't know what he would think. He might not like you around me at all." She turned away from him, so he couldn't see her fall apart.

Jax came up behind her and wrapped his arms around her waist. "If he loved you half as much as you said he did, and I don't know how he couldn't, he'd want me to protect you with my life."

Brynn tensed but said nothing. She closed her eyes and wished Nate would give her a sign. A loud banging noise occurred over head, sending Jax running from the room. She stood frozen to the floor. Could Apollo, or his gang, be here already?

A dignified voice spoke behind her. "I only have a moment, before he concludes the ladder fell from the breeze of an open window."

"Sebastian, you scared the daylights out of me. What are you doing?" she asked in a low tone.

"You should let that young man help you. Don't be proud. Pride can cost you everything. Take it on good authority."

"I'm not living with him."

"Of course not. That wouldn't be proper. You shall live here, and I will watch over you while he is not present."

"Why would you do that? You barely know me."

"You remind me of my wife, Helena. I should have done more for her."

"What are you talking about?"

Sebastian looked toward the hallway and faded away just moments before Jax entered. "A ladder fell. Someone left the window open. It's only thirty degrees out there. I'm going to have to talk to Mike when he gets here. You're not going to want to heat the outside…" He stopped talking, before adding… "You're looking at me like I've grown another nose."

Brynn looked past Jax to where Sebastian stood, nodding his head. She returned the nod, ever so slightly. "You're right. I'll let you help me, but I'm not moving in with you," she added quickly. "I will agree to the security system. I'll agree to let you take the lead while we're here, and let you accompany me any place after dark, but that's it."

"And you'll allow me to pick you up and take you home while you're staying at the inn." She started to object when he spoke over her. "And before I leave you, I check out your room."

Sebastian walked over to where Jax had been sanding, inspecting his work with a swipe of his finger. "I like this young man. He's a very good negotiator. He would have been an asset to my company…and he's very good with a piece of sandpaper."

Brynn's head fell back in frustration. She wanted to tell the friendly ghost to zip it, but Jax would think she'd lost her mind.

"So, do we have a deal?" he asked.

"Take it, my dear, it's the best you're going to get."

She glared past Jax to where Sebastian stood with a hand resting in his suit coat, looking dignified.

"Why are you shooting daggers at the wall?"

"Would you believe I'm shooting them at Sebastian Morgan?"

Jax laughed. "Nice try."

"What? The young man doesn't believe in ghosts? Maybe, I'll have to convince him." Sebastian moved in the direction of Jax.

“That wouldn’t be a good idea.”

“What wouldn’t?”

“Nothing. Did you have anything you wanted to go over before I head upstairs?” she asked.

“As a matter of fact, I do, but I am curious what keeps you going upstairs to the attic.”

She smiled mischievously. “Treasure hunt.” That sounded better than *I’m planning the renovations with a dead guy.* “So, what did you need to discuss?”

“This area needs a lot of work before it’s livable.”

Brynn interrupted. “I told you I just need a place to crash, so I can move in.”

“Hear me out. What if we clean up the dining area and we could bring in your bed, a chair, lamp…whatever to make you comfortable? The plumber has the downstairs bathroom workable. That would give me the time to do this right, and you could still move in.”

“I guess it would work, but I really don’t need some fancy space, if that’s what’s holding you up.”

“I want you to have a fancy space.”

“I could help you. I can use sandpaper.”

“And you would expect a discount?” He folded his arms across his chest in mock appraisal.

“Naturally.” She grinned. “And thank you, Jax. I do appreciate all you’ve done for me.”

“You’re welcome. Now, go…do whatever you do in the attic. I’ll have a piece of sandpaper ready when you return.” He bent over and picked a piece off the floor, kneeling down in front of the baseboard.

Brynn studied him momentarily. What was Jax Maddox really like? He couldn’t be this nice.

"You're attracted to him."

She stifled a groan. This ghost was really starting to get on her nerves. And she couldn't comment around Jax, so she made a beeline for the attic where she could really give him a piece of her mind. No one was on the second floor to hear her. Mike and his crew had another job this morning. Casper was going to get an earful.

Reaching the top step, Brynn waited for Sebastian to appear. He didn't disappoint. "He's a good-looking young man. I can understand the attraction, and you're of marriageable age. I would say, a little beyond perhaps?"

"I am *not* attracted to him." It was difficult to yell when all you could do was whisper. "And are you saying I'm old?" Her hands went to her hips.

"I understand you were married before?"

"You're not only a ghost, but you eavesdrop?"

"I pay attention to detail, my dear. That is how I was successful. Now, what is this about you being in danger?"

Brynn could hardly believe she was explaining her life story to someone who lived a century before her, but Sebastian Morgan was becoming very real to her. She concluded her story with a "there you have it."

He nodded once and rubbed his chin without responding right away. "I guess I've missed some things in this old castle. This world sounds like an undignified place. What is a drugs and weapons ring?"

"Illegal drugs, or weapons, that are sold on the black market. These dealers get loads of money from their sales, and people are dying from addiction. And the weapons...they would boggle your mind. It's not nineteen hundred anymore."

"It would seem not. Remind me not to venture out. However, here I will help you."

"How?"

"I was quite known for my intelligence and problem solving ability. Together we will figure out what these hooligans are looking for."

His offer touched her. "I'll take you up on that. My things should arrive by the end of the week from New York. Whatever they're after, if I have it, will be in the boxes they deliver."

"Are you intending on filling my home with tacky furniture?"

Brynn laughed. "I only kept my bed and my favorite reading chair. The rest is boxes of books and personal items. I wanted to start new here."

"And so you shall, my dear, so you shall."

Chapter Seventeen

After Brynn's conversation with Sebastian, she spent the morning sanding woodwork in what would be her living room. They talked about everything from politics to their childhoods. She found she had much in common with Jaxson Maddox.

She told him of her plans for the bed and breakfast and what she hoped to accomplish. His ideas were good ones, and she appreciated another viewpoint. The carriage house renovation was discussed, and Brynn's excitement grew. This place could really be something. And she had a feeling Jax was going to be a part of that success. He was the male perspective she lacked.

It was lunch before she realized. "I have to get going," she announced.

"Where? We're not done."

"I have a meeting." She swiped the dirt from the knees of her jeans.

"With?"

"Kinda nosey, aren't you?" she grinned.

"We have an agreement, sunshine. You tell me where you're going, so I can watch out for you."

Brynn attempted to keep hidden the effect his endearment had on her. "It's broad daylight. Anyway, if you must know, I have an appointment with Brad Shuller at the furniture store."

"Brad? Casanova Brad?" His eyes narrowed.

"I take it you don't like him."

"Give me a minute to clean up. I'm going with you."

"Really, Jax, that's not necessary." She grabbed her purse from the corner.

"He'll be all over you," he replied grumpily.

"I doubt that. I need to get out and meet some people from the community, and having you sit across from him and snarl won't get me a discount."

"So, how do you intend on getting a discount?" His mood wasn't improving.

"I'll pretend you didn't say that. I'll call you when I'm safely home. Promise."

He grumbled something unintelligible and grabbed the sandpaper.

"You have a pouty face."

He stopped what he was doing, and looked up at her with a look that stopped her in her tracks. He cared about her, and she wasn't taking him seriously. Guilt replaced humor. "I'm sorry, Jax, I'll be careful. And if I get into something I can't handle, you'll be the first person I call."

"And I'll be there."

"I know you will. I'll call you later."

Brynn walked to her car and looked up to the window that always gave her the willies. There stood Sebastian. She waved, and he nodded, then disappeared. She positioned herself behind the wheel, all the while questioning her sanity. Did Sebastian really exist as a ghost, or was she traumatized and creating imaginary friends? No one else could see, or hear him. She pushed all thoughts of ghosts aside and concentrated on the next step in her renovation—

furniture. It would take time to order and arrive. She knew this from experience.

Brynn pulled into the parking lot of Shuller Furniture without incident. Jax was pretty worked up about this meeting. She wondered what kind of person this Brad Shuller was. She reached in the back for her briefcase and figured there was no time like the present to find out. He wouldn't be the first flirt she'd dealt with.

The store was large and impressive. The furniture inside its walls, most likely, wouldn't be what she was looking for. Brynn's vision was more old-world Edwardian with comfort. Hopefully, she could keep her patronage in town.

"Can I help you?"

"I have a meeting with Mr. Shuller. My name's Brynn Austin."

The salesman scurried off. Brynn took the opportunity to look over the inventory.

"Ms. Austin? Brad Shuller. Come on back to my office. I hope you haven't been waiting long."

She answered the customary small talk with, "No, not at all. I just arrived." Brynn followed him toward the back of the store and through a warehouse before entering a large office with modern décor. The stainless steel and polished black furniture grabbed her attention. The gray walls and simple lines, which were carried through to the artwork around the room, impressed her. He knew what he was doing, or someone in his employ was talented. Either way he had gained some points with her. However, she couldn't lay it on too thick. Brynn, also, knew the art of negotiation. "Nicely done. Back in New York, I was an interior designer. I appreciate detail."

"Please, sit. Thank you. I appreciate beauty myself."

Jax's words echoed in the back of her mind. And she wasn't expecting Brad Shuller to be drop dead gorgeous either. The dark, designer suit complemented his dark hair and eyes. He had the whole monochromatic thing going on, and it suited him. It gave him an air of mystery.

He interrupted her thoughts. "What can I help you with?" The sultry way he spoke the words increased her already rapidly beating heartbeat.

"I'm restoring Sebastian's Castle, and my intent is to turn it into a bed and breakfast. I'd like to use furniture inspired by the Italian Renaissance, the Elizabethan era, the French Empire…you get the idea. But it has to be comfortable and inviting. My plan is to theme the rooms. I want my guests to feel they've entered a fairy tale when they first walk in. Do you think you can help me accomplish that?"

"I'd love to, and I'm up for a challenge. Of course, we'd have to spend some time together pouring over catalogs."

His comments were just innocent enough to keep her guessing. "Good. I have some sketches drawn, but I'd like to improve on them, and go over my color scheme before we set up another meeting." They bounced ideas back in forth for a short time, before she glanced at her watch and said, "I won't take up any more of your time today." She stood and reached her hand out to his. "I'll be in touch."

He placed a kiss on the back of her hand. The heat of the intimate gesture spread to her face. This guy was smooth.

"I'll look forward to spending time with such a beautiful woman." He walked around his desk and placed a hand on her back, guiding her to the door. "I would be honored to take you to dinner."

"I'm flattered, Mr. Shuller, but I'm very busy keeping this project on schedule."

"A business dinner, perhaps?"

"I'd really rather keep the tongues from wagging. I'm new in town, and I'd like my reputation to be, well, on the respectable side."

"I understand. We'll keep it respectable. Drop by anytime with your drawings. I look forward to seeing them, and you."

Jax wasn't far off base with this one. Ignoring the flirtatious comment, she exited the office with a flushed face. Admittedly, she wasn't immune to his charm.

Brynn made it to her car in record time. She really hoped she could tame the flirtatious furniture salesman. She didn't need another complication. While reaching up to adjust her rearview mirror, she noticed a car parked behind her. A man sat in the front seat with a newspaper in front of his face. She couldn't get a clean view. Brynn was sure it was the paranoia again, but she couldn't risk ignoring anything.

She pulled out into traffic, and so did the car behind her. She made some bogus turns down a couple of the busier streets. The car remained a short distance behind her. The blood thumped in her ears, and her stomach rolled with dread. She was being followed. She stopped at the light and pushed Jax's number.

"Hey, sunshine, are you done with Casanova?"

Relief washed over her just hearing his voice. "Jax,

I think I'm being followed."

His voice turned serious. "Okay, honey, tell me where you're at. Are you close to the castle?"

"Yes, but I don't want to lead anyone there." She had to keep a clear head.

"I'm in my truck. Tell me where you are." She gave him the street names. "I want you to go to the police station. I'm going to meet you there. Keep your doors locked. I shouldn't be but a few minutes behind you."

"Jax, I don't know where the station is." Panicking was not an option. She stole a look in the mirror. They were still behind her.

He gave her quick directions and made her repeat them. "Stay on the phone with me. Don't hang up, got it?"

Within minutes she pulled up in front of the police station, and the car drove right on by. "They kept going."

"Did you get a description of the car? A license plate number?"

"A description, yes, but only the first three letters of the license plate."

"I'm behind you."

Brynn jumped out of the car and walked to him at breakneck speed. He pulled her into an embrace. "You're shaking."

"I probably over-reacted." She stepped back, suddenly aware that someone might have seen the display of affection, and get the wrong idea.

"Trust your instincts. How long did they follow you?" He pulled her with him to the sidewalk.

"About five minutes. I didn't want them to follow

me home, but they're going to figure out where I live. It's only a matter of time."

His face turned grim. Gone was the smile in his eyes. "Let's go inside and file a report. And I think you should call that detective in New York too."

She nodded. He was right. She had more to worry about than a ghost in the attic.

Chapter Eighteen

Brynn sat across from a uniformed police officer. To her right sat Jax. She explained the last year of her life, along with the phone call from Detective Wainwright. A report was filed, and a phone call made to the NYPD.

The officer hung up looking grim. "Mrs. Austin, do you live alone?"

"Yes, why?" She shifted in her chair.

"Detective Wainwright believes it might be wise if you're not alone, and that maybe you should stay with a friend. I tend to agree with him. At this time, I can't put you under police protection, because I have no proof that there's a threat." His attention turned to Jax. "Are you the boyfriend?"

"He's my contractor." Brynn cut Jax off before he could speak. "I'm staying at the inn until I'm able to move into the castle. I'm surrounded by people," she quickly added.

"I strongly suggest you don't venture out by yourself, until this whole thing is wrapped up."

Whole thing? Her husband was murdered over this *whole thing.* "I understand. I'll be very careful. Are we free to go?"

The officer chuckled. "We aren't holding you here, Mrs. Austin. Be careful, and if you have any concerns, or anything else happens to spook you, give us a call."

Brynn stood and reached out her hand. "Thank you. I will."

The officer stood and shook Jax's hand. "You know what I would do if she was in my orbit?"

"Not let her out of your sight?"

"Exactly. You both have a good evening."

Brynn huffed with impatience on her way out the door. "Let's talk about the lady like she's not standing there."

"Brynn, stop." Jax's voice held a sternness she'd never heard before.

She swung around to face him. "What?"

His voice softened. "Don't be too proud to ask me for help."

Jax's concerned expression threw all anger out the door. Her shoulders slumped. She was already tired of the fight, and it hadn't even really begun. She wanted to be normal again. He opened the car door and waited for her to slide behind the wheel. "I'm following you back to your place, and then I'm going to walk you up, and check your room. No arguments."

She simply nodded. He wasn't making her admit she was scared as hell, and as alone as anyone could feel.

****

Jax followed her the short distance to the inn. His senses were heightened as he watched her in front of him. All this guy had to do was slip up one time when he was around… "Damn!" He pounded the steering wheel. He wanted to scoop her up and take her back to his place, but she would never go for that. So, he had to settle with a search of her room and hope for the best. Or did he?

He parked behind her and walked to her car. She stepped out without a word. Was it his imagination, or did she look pale?

"You sure you want to stay here? I have plenty of room at my place."

"Thanks for the offer, but who knows how long this will go on. I have to learn to take care of myself."

"I could stay here." Jax knew before the words left his mouth, she would never agree.

She shook her head firmly. "No. I'll agree to a sweep of my room, but that's it. The staff is here…other guests. I'll be fine—really."

The rest of the walk to her room was short on conversation. Plenty of thoughts going through his head, like why did everything have to be so damned difficult? He could tell she was attracted to him, but she was devoted to her husband—even in death. He'd have to be patient. Hell, he wasn't in any hurry. He'd gone this long without a relationship. Yeah, but he'd never met someone like Brynn before—someone with substance, guts, and intelligence to complement the beautiful face—among other things.

They arrived at her door, and he waited for her to retrieve the key. She grabbed the handle, and he stopped her before she entered. "Remember the deal?" She sighed and stepped aside. "Wait here," he ordered.

He could see through the room and out the back window. The lamplights outside showcased the snow falling at a fast pace. Winter still had a strong grip. Jax flipped on the light and jumped back. "Damn cat." He returned the hiss Romeo threw at him. It only took a few minutes to check around. There wasn't too many places to hide, and he'd checked them all. He leaned against the door jam. "What are you still doing out here?"

"Funny. I told you it would be fine." Brynn breezed by, and her perfume hung in the air around him.

He moved to the window to close the blind. A shadow below caught his attention, but he made no outward notice of it. "Brynn, shut out the light."

She followed his directive, but asked, "What do you see?"

"Maybe nothing." A man stood on the wharf shadowed in the darkness. Jax would have missed him if it hadn't been for the glow of his cigarette. He focused, not taking his eyes off of him. He couldn't tell if he was watching Brynn's room, but he was facing in this direction.

The silence weighed heavily in the room. He knew she waited for an explanation. The man moved closer, still he couldn't make out his face. He looked up to the room, and Jax slowly let go of the slats he held open. He moved away from the window, not knowing what the interloper's intention was. "Your room's being watched."

Brynn started past him, and he grasped her arm. "No, sunshine. Not safe."

She bit down on her lower lip, nodded, and lowered herself on the couch. The look of defeat in her posture angered him.

He started for the door, and she jumped up and grabbed him with a wild panic in her eyes. "No! You can't go out there!"

"I'm just going to go out there and find out why he's hanging around."

"You can't." Her desperation stopped him. "The people that did this to Nate..." She paused. "They'll come after you. I can't..."

He framed her face with his hands, searching her eyes with a tenderness he'd never experienced before. "You can't what, Brynn?"

"I can't be responsible for you getting hurt...or worse."

He was fairly certain that wasn't what she was going to say.

"You're either coming home with me, or I'm staying here. I won't take no for an answer."

"People will talk."

"You're more worried about what people will say, than the possibility that whoever murdered your husband may be watching you?" He couldn't put a lid on his irritation. And, yeah, maybe that was a little blunt.

He reached for his cell and called the police. She wasn't going to dictate how he handled this, because she was afraid of some small town gossip.

The officers arrived in minutes and searched the area. They hadn't spotted anyone in the immediate vicinity that matched the description, but they did find a couple of cigarette butts right where Jax had spotted the interloper. They promised to keep an eye out and file a report.

Jax understood little could be done. No contact had been made. His gut feeling kicked in, and it wasn't a good one. "I'm going down to my truck, and get a change of clothes." She wasn't changing his mind.

Brynn stood at the window, peeking out the blinds. Her body language screamed fear. She could argue all she wanted, but he was staying.

Her response shocked him. "Please, be careful."

"I will. Don't open the door unless you hear my voice. Got it?"

Brynn nodded, never leaving her post at the window. She stared at the falling snow and inhaled a shaky breath. Her husband's killer was out there. Was she next?

Chapter Nineteen

Brynn's focus struggled with the darkness outside her window. She glanced at her clock. Jax had been gone too long. Her heart thumped in her chest, as she paced. Finally, his long-awaited voice came from the other side of the door, and she opened it quickly. "What took you so long?" Then, it dawned on her. "You went searching for him, didn't you?"

"I took a quick look around." He dropped a small duffel bag on the bed, and she was suddenly very aware of his proximity. Her heart thumped for a different reason.

Brynn moved back to the window to put distance between them. "So, you carry clothes in your truck?" Why did she ask that? She stifled a groan.

"I, sometimes, have meetings with clients mid-day and don't like to go with sawdust and dirt on me. It's easier than running home."

Brynn glanced in his direction and didn't miss the smirk cross his face. A change of subject was in order. She leaned against the wall, keeping her vigil at the window. "You could have gotten ambushed out there."

"I know what I'm doing." She didn't have to see him moving toward her. The electricity flying between them was telling enough. Her arm tingled under his touch. "You can't stand there all night." He led her to the couch and grabbed the anchor-covered quilt hanging on the back. "Sit," he commanded, and wrapped the cover around her.

Jax angled himself next to her, his arm resting dangerously close to touching her. "I don't want you putting yourself in danger, because of me. You shouldn't even be here."

"Why shouldn't I be here?"

"Do you want the entire list?" When he didn't respond, she nervously filled the silence. "The top reason is I'm not your…"

"Responsibility," he finished for her. "I've made you my responsibility, whether you like it or not. I don't let friends down. I know a little about self-defense, and I'm going to watch over you. No more arguments, so you might as well drop the subject. And before you say it, I don't care what people think. I care that you're safe. Anyway, would it be so bad if people thought you liked me?"

She hadn't meant to insult him. In her heart, she was still Nate's wife, and having anyone think she was sleeping with Jax…well, the idea horrified her. She'd been in town such a short time, and she knew how fast gossip spread. "It's not that I'd be embarrassed of being with you." Her mouth went dry. "I don't want anyone to think I've moved on."

"Why, Brynn?"

"Because…because, I love my husband. And if I move on, he's really gone." The tears dampened her face. She couldn't hide the emotions any longer.

Jax pulled her close while the tears flowed freely. She swiped at her face, and pulled back. "I'm sorry."

"About?"

He infuriated her, at times, with his simple

questions. She sighed. What was she sorry for? She collected her thoughts before finally speaking. "I'm sorry I draggedyou into this. I'm sorry I can't be the person you want me to be. And most of all, I'm sorry I seem so ungrateful, because I'm not."

The tender eyes and soft smile made her wish he could be more. The timing sucked, and there was nothing she could do about that. She was doing everything possible to hold on to Nate, and he was slipping away. If she let Jax into her life, into her heart, she knew without a doubt she would no longer be Mrs. Nathaniel Austin.

"Tell me what you're thinking."

"Every day that separates me from Nate's last day is a day he's farther from me." She sucked in her lower lip with an attempt to keep it together. The words…how did she find the words?

"Go on."

"It's been over a year since I buried him. Every day that passes I forget things." This was so hard.

"Like?"

"Like the sound of his voice. The things that made him laugh. The smell of his cologne. So many things. It's like he's fading away from me, and I don't want to forget. I loved him. He's my husband." She looked into Jax's eyes. "How can I forget these things about the man I loved?"

He pulled her to his side, and gently stroked her head. "I don't know anything about this kind of loss, but I'm learning. You have good memories with him?"

"The best."

"Then I'd say, you'll never forget him. He's always going to be a part of your life. Something will spark a memory, and he'll return. And my guess is you'll be able to smile at the memories someday."

"Don't you see? That's why I'll never be able to move on with someone else. Who'd want to compete with a dead husband?"

"Me," he answered.

"Jax…"

He interrupted her. "Enough heavy talk for now. We don't have to label this. You know I'm crazy about you, and I know you need time and space. Why don't I start a fire, and we'll watch a movie?"

"That sounds great." Anything to get her mind off of everything going on around her.

"Do you mind if I get a shower? You can find something for us to watch."

The thought of him using her shower seemed intimate. Her mind wandered, and she immediately pulled it back. The thoughts drifting through her brain had no right to be there.

Jax started the fire before disappearing into the bathroom. She grabbed a sweatshirt and a pair of yoga pants and changed while the shower ran. She fed Romeo, put her clothes away, and walked to the window. The glow of one small light on the desk didn't illuminate the room much. She could have one peek. She slid her fingers between the slats. There was no one on the wharf at this hour, but the snow fell heavily. Nights like this, back in Brooklyn, she and Nate would take a walk. Now, she didn't feel safe enough to leave her room.

"Brynn, please stay away from the window." She jumped at Jax's voice behind her. "We don't know who we're dealing with yet."

She nodded and joined him on the couch. His short haircut fit him. The dampness of his hair made it look three shades darker than the light brown she'd grown accustomed to. He wore a navy blue polo shirt with *Maddox Construction* embroidered over the left side. The muscles of his biceps spilled out of the sleeves.

"Brynn? Did you hear me?"

"I'm sorry. No. What did you say?"

"I asked what you wanted to watch."

He didn't seem to notice her embarrassment, and thank God he couldn't read her thoughts. She didn't want to encourage him.

He grabbed the remote. "Do you like old movies?"

"Love them." Again, she was reminded of evenings spent with Nate. In many ways, Jax had much in common with her husband.

The fire was stoked, the TV was turned to a classic movie station, and the snow fell outside the window. The atmosphere couldn't have been any more romantic. Well, that's what she thought, until Jax pulled her close and covered them with the quilt. He put his arm around her but made no other move. She tensed at the closeness but soon relaxed. For once, she wasn't going to read too much into it. Brynn needed strong arms around her.

Chapter Twenty

After the movie ended, they pulled out the sofa bed and grabbed blankets and an extra pillow for Jax. Brynn climbed into her bed and turned off the bedside lamp. The lights from the wharf shined softly in the room, and Jax could make out her silhouette. It had been a great evening between them, and he made some progress tonight. She had relaxed.

"Night, Brynn."

"Night, John Boy."

Her giggle traveled through the darkness to his ears, and he smiled.

Jax wasn't exactly sure what jolted him awake a short time later, but his attention immediately shot to the door. The handle jiggled ever so slightly. He jumped up and moved to Brynn's side. He whispered, and she bolted upright. He motioned for her silence, then crossed the room, waiting to the side of the door. Jax thought about throwing the door open and having the element of surprise but decided the element of surprise would be better used hiding in the shadows of a dark room. He had no idea if this had anything to do with Nate's murder. He was better off to assume it did.

The adrenaline pumped through his veins. His gun was in his duffel bag across the room. He could handle this hand to hand if there wasn't a group of them. Damn! Too late to go for the gun. The door inched open allowing the hall light to seep in. Jax pushed himself tight against the wall and prayed Brynn wouldn't panic and alert the intruder.

The door opened the rest of the way, and Jax made his move throwing a chokehold around a good-sized man. The intruder struggled, and Jax tightened his grip until he had him to the ground with his arm in a painful position. "Brynn, turn the light on and call 9-1-1."

The man squirmed on the floor saying, "Let go of me, man. I had the wrong room. That's all."

"Sure you did, and you just happened to have a key that opened the door?" Brynn hung up, and Jax looked in her direction. "Do you know this guy?"

"No, dude. I forgot my key and picked the lock."

"Shut up!" He ordered. "Have you ever seen this guy before?"

Brynn was white as a ghost, but answered firmly. "No, never."

He didn't buy the story of the forgotten key and the wrong room. Jax guessed he was the one watching from outside earlier, but he'd let the police ask the questions.

"Brynn, get that chair and sit it right here." Jax brought the guy up in a standing position and lowered him roughly to the chair. He got a better look at him, and he wasn't as old as he thought—maybe twenty. "What's your name, kid?"

"I'm not here to hurt anyone." Jax threw him a cynical look. "Really. I'm not. I have something that needed delivered."

"What are you talking about?"

"It's in my coat pocket."

Jax eyed him suspiciously, and it was apparent Brynn was thinking the same. "Be careful, Jax," she warned.

He patted the guy down, searching for weapons. He was clean "Reach into your coat pocket very slowly." Jax had the other arm twisted behind him. If he made a move, he wouldn't think twice before breaking it.

The door to the hallway was still ajar, and a commotion from below reached Jax's ears. Two uniformed officers and the night manager stood in the doorway seconds later.

"Having some trouble tonight, folks?"

Jax glanced over to where Brynn stood. He knew she had to be horrified. She hadn't wanted him to stay, and now the manager and two city officers were privy to the information. He refused to be sorry. God knows what would have happened if he hadn't been here.

"Yeah. Woke up to this braniac picking the lock. He found me waiting to greet him. Told me, just now, he had a delivery." Jax held up the envelope.

"I swear I wasn't going to hurt anyone. Some guy gave me a hundred dollars to leave this in the room. I've been off work for a while and…"

"You thought you'd do a little breaking and entering." The officer helped the guy out of the chair and handcuffed him. "What's in the envelope?" he asked Jax.

Brynn stood at Jax's side while he opened it. He pulled out a gift certificate to the pub. "What the hell? You broke in here to leave a gift certificate?"

"Dude, I didn't know what was in the envelope. The guy just said it was important."

"Could you identify this guy if you saw him again," the officer asked.

"I don't know. Maybe. I really wasn't paying much attention to what he looked like."

"I'll take him out to the cruiser," he said to his partner. "You can get the scoop for the report. Ma'am?" The officer addressed the manager. "If you don't have anything to add, you're free to go back downstairs."

"No, I'm sorry. I didn't see a thing. I didn't even see him walk past the front desk. How did you get in here?" She glared at the guy in cuffs.

"Back door, off the wharf," he replied with a grin. That solidified Jax's theory of him watching the room.

"That door's locked," the manager replied stiffly.

"Not anymore."

The room cleared out after that, and Jax and Brynn ran down the story with the remaining officer—from the call earlier about the suspicious man outside, to the danger Brynn might be in. The officer took careful notes, and before long he was gone too.

They stood alone in the room, and Jax spoke first. "I'm sorry, sunshine. I know you didn't want anyone to know I was here."

He waited, for what seemed minutes, for her to speak. "I'm glad you were here. I don't know how well I would have handled that." She paused with an uncertain look. "Are you a cop, Jax?"

Her husband must have taught her well. "Sort of," was all he said.

"You know, you'll have to do better than that?"

"I was in the Military Police Corps."

"Really?"

"Yeah. Really. For eight years. I picked up a thing or two." He picked up more than a thing or two, but that part of his life was over. "What gave it away?"

"I was suspicious the day we were alone, and you searched the castle. You moved like Nate would have."

"I'll take that as a compliment. Old habits…" he trailed off. Awkward silence followed. "We still have a few hours of dark. Why don't you try to get some sleep?"

She nodded. "Why would anyone pay someone to break in here and leave a gift certificate?"

"I have my theories."

"Like?"

He sat on the bed next to her. Her body tensed immediately, but he ignored it. "They're either trying to lure you away, so they can search the room, or they want to try to get you alone. They're going to have a hard time with the last one."

"I'm glad you were here."

"Me too, sunshine. Get some sleep." He couldn't help himself. He kissed her on the forehead, before heading back to the cold sofa bed.

Chapter Twenty-One

Brynn rolled over and stared at the ceiling. Anything was better than seeing Jax's silhouette in the darkness. He made her feel things—things she didn't want to feel. A thousand thoughts bounced around her brain. He had been a cop…a different kind of cop, but still a cop. Was she naturally attracted to them? She pushed the absurd thought from her mind, only to have it be replaced with another one.

Her mind twisted and turned, finally stopping at the intruder. What was the reason behind the gift certificate? If Apollo was behind this, and she believed he was, he had a reason. She would be smarter than him. She was going to find out what Nate had on him, and end this. He was going to pay for the murder of her husband. And no one was going to stop her. Not even a sexy contractor with ninja moves.

****

They awoke to four inches of freshly fallen snow. The river was a beautiful back drop to the fluffy snow hanging on to every flat surface. Brynn showered and came out to coffee and breakfast.

Jax had everything sitting out on the little table in her room. "That smells delicious. I'm starved." He pulled out the chair for her, and her heart softened just a little bit more.

"Thanks," she muttered.

"So what's on our agenda today?" he asked, buttering a piece of toast.

"What do you mean 'our'?"

"I'm not letting you out of my sight, remember?"

"Well, then, I suppose I'll be going to the castle, so you can work." She sighed at the first bite of scrambled eggs.

"Did you have anything else planned?"

"I planned on scrubbing down the walls of the dining room. My things are being delivered tomorrow."

"And you plan on staying there?"

"Of course. You knew that."

He wiped his lips with a napkin before speaking. "Our first order of business will be getting you a security system. You're not staying there until it's installed."

"You do realize I don't have to obey your every command?" She appreciated his concern, but he wasn't her lord and master.

"I'm going to keep you safe, and for me to do that you're going to have to listen to me."

That stern tone in his voice returned. She was going to argue, but then thought better of it. "Okay. I get it. Nate would say those very words to me. I know he would. And I know he'd want me to listen. One thing you need to understand, I'm going to find out what they're after, and I'm going to make sure Apollo Banks pays with his life."

"As long as you know I'll be by your side while you do it."

"Don't get in my way."

"Don't do anything stupid, and I won't."

His eyes pierced hers during the exchange, and she

looked away first. "I'm going to finish my breakfast."

The chuckle from across the table sent her heart fluttering. She closed her eyes at the thought she'd been avoiding. Jax Maddox was her second chance. She just didn't think she wanted a second chance.

They went about their business after breakfast. He closed up the sofa bed, folding the blankets, and setting the pillow on top. She collected her drawings and notes and placed them in her briefcase. She lowered her coat from the hook, and Jax was by her side, taking it from her before she could stop him. He held it open, and she shoved an arm in. It was really hard to deny her feelings when he continuously did this kind of stuff.

He donned his coat and pulled the stocking cap out of the pocket. She tried not to stare at everything he did. He fascinated her, and the attraction was no longer deniable.

Brynn shoved her hands in her pockets, searching for her car keys. She came out empty handed. The search in her purse also produced negative results.

"What are you looking for?" he asked.

"My keys. I can't remember where I put them."

He held them up. "They were on the desk."

"Oh, good. Thanks." She held out her hand, but he shoved them in his pocket. "What are you doing?"

"You don't need these until we get back later. I'm driving." He opened the door and made a sweeping motion for her to pass.

"I'm perfectly capable of…"

"Yeah, I know, sunshine—taking care of yourself. Let's go."

She exhaled a nice, hearty breath of frustration before passing him. There was no use arguing. They were going to the same place.

The snow was deeper than she'd expected. Jax had already warmed up the truck and cleaned the windows. She had to admit the drive to the castle went far better in a four-wheel drive truck than her car. They turned down the lane, and she immediately noticed it was plowed.

"Who plowed?"

"I called a buddy of mine this morning and had him take care of it."

"I never thought about it. How much? I'll pay you back." She opened her purse.

He reached over and laid a hand over hers. "You owe me nothing." He was ready for the argument, so he added, "I'll add it on your bill."

"You better."

Brynn jumped out of the truck and looked up to the sky. The snow just wouldn't stop. She glanced up to the window, but Sebastian wasn't there. In her search to find her ghost, she hadn't noticed Mike standing by the door until they were on top of him. He stared at them strangely, before uttering a "hello".

"Morning, Mike," Jax said cheerily. "Sorry I'm running late. Stopped to pick Brynn up. I thought maybe she'd have some trouble in the snow."

Another reason to fall hard for this guy. Now, he was protecting her reputation.

"Right," Mike commented, like their arrival together finally made sense. "Mornin', little lady. I was working on the wiring for this doorbell. It's ancient. I know you want to keep to a certain theme here, but would you mind something a little newer?"

Brynn laughed. "I think I can make a concession

with the doorbell, but take that doorknocker down, and we're going to rumble."

"Well, we have ourselves a deal then."

Jax maneuvered around Mike and opened the door for them. Brynn sighed at the warmth. The old lighting was slowly being replaced with new fixtures, but with an antique feel. She approved.

"I'm going to give the security company a call, and see if they can come out today." Jax was already moving down the hall with phone in hand.

That gave her time to find Sebastian. He wasn't making an appearance in the attic, so she entered the bedroom she'd always spotted him in. "Sebastian?"

"Right here, my lady."

Brynn smiled as his image appeared. "I thought you'd be in the attic."

"This is much more civilized, don't you think?"

"It is, but I have to be careful no one hears me, or they'll think I've gone nuts."

"Nuts? What do nuts have to do with you being careful?"

It was easy to forget she was talking to a ghost that lived in the turn of the twentieth century. "It's an expression meaning crazy."

"Ahhh. Because they'll think you're talking to yourself?" He didn't wait for a reply. "I could always make an appearance."

"You can control that?"

"I don't know. I've never tried. You're the only one that I've been able to communicate with. I wonder why that's so?"

"Listen, Sebastian, I have some things to tell you."

He turned from the window and looked her way.

"You sound worried, my dear, have you trouble?"

"I'm not sure." She went on to tell him about her unexpected visitor at the inn, the car following her, and the conversations with the Mystic police department, and the NYPD detective. They don't think I should be alone."

"Yes, you should move in as quickly as possible. I will keep a close eye. You said your new fellow was getting a security system? I really don't relish the thought of dogs in the house, but if we must…"

She ignored the comment about Jax being her new fellow, and moved on to an explanation of the security system. "No, not dogs. It's electronic. If someone trips the alarm, the police are called."

"Trips? Oh, dear me. The rugs are quite old. Are you having them replaced?"

"If someone breaks into the castle, the system notifies the police department."

His eyebrows drew together, and she could barely see the wrinkling of his forehead as he faded in and out. "How does it accomplish that?"

"I'm not sure the mechanics of it. Let's just say modern technology."

He nodded in agreement. "You don't need all that poppycock. I'll take care of any interlopers."

"And how will you do that?" She bit down on the grin threatening to spread across her face.

"I'll scare them, of course. I am a ghost, or have you forgotten?"

"I quite remember. I believe I'm the one that informed you." The smile was free. "Jax is watching out for me, and the security system will be a plus."

"Your young man doesn't intend on residing here,

does he? Because, that would not be proper. I couldn't allow it."

"No. He's not staying here. I have to say, Sebastian, I was a little nervous moving in to this huge place by myself. I'll enjoy your company."

"Likewise, my lady. It's been a long time, since I've had anyone to talk to."

She smiled at his approval. "Good. Now, I've brought some sketches for you to look over. I have some ideas for this room, and I want your input. I'm guessing this was your room?"

"Yes, yes…Helena's chambers were next door. What do you have there?" He hovered over the plans she'd laid out on a piece of plywood set upon wooden horses. Brynn stood next to him.

"Brynn, were you talking to someone?" She jumped at Jax's voice behind her.

How was she going to get out of this one?

Chapter Twenty-Two

"I, um, yeah, I was talking to the movers."

"What are you doing in here?"

"The lighting is good. I thought I'd work on my drawings. Is there a problem?" She had to throw him on the defensive.

"No. I get a little nervous when I can't find you…considering the circumstances." He glanced around the room suspiciously.

Brynn was amazed that Sebastian could be so obviously standing beside her, and Jax couldn't see him. She wondered why. "Well, now you know where I am."

"Okay. I'll be downstairs." He glanced around the room one last time.

"Great. Thank you."

Brynn closed the door behind him and whispered to Sebastian, "I guess I'll have to be more careful."

Sebastian switched the topic of conversation back to her scare the night before. "It seems we would both have a mystery in our lives. I've been considering the possibility of my remaining here due to unfinished business. It's intriguing to think I might be able to move on from these circumstances. But where would I move on to?"

Brynn didn't believe the question was one he wanted her to answer, but one he needed to answer for himself. “I still have your wife’s journal. Would you like to read it?”

“I wouldn’t want to betray her trust.”

“If it helps bring you back to her, I’m sure she’d be fine with it.”

“Do you really think so?”

“I do.” She pulled the journal from her briefcase and laid it on the makeshift table, next to her plans. “I’ll leave it here, and you can decide.”

He nodded firmly, not showing the emotion that had to be plaguing him. He cleared his throat and said, “Now, how do we figure out what these men are after? We need to put our heads together. Maybe we need to let them in the castle.”

“Let them in? You can’t be serious.” When he didn’t confess to a joke, she continued, “That would be dangerous. These men killed Nate.”

“Dangerous to you, perhaps, but not to me. They can’t kill someone who’s already deceased.”

Well, he had a point.

“You, naturally, would not be in residence when the permitted breaking and entering occurs.”

“Do you have a plan, Sebastian?”

“Not yet, my dear, but I’m working on it. Let us continue with these plans of yours for now, shall we?”

****

Jax wondered what she was up to. Her behavior was odd at best. He attempted to ignore the niggling in the back of his brain by making a few phone calls. The security company would arrive in an hour or so. He had to have that in place before she moved in. He knew staying with her was not on option. She would never allow it.

Whenever she walked into this place, she seemed distracted. And she always disappeared to the attic. Now, today, he'd found her in an upstairs bedroom, and he swore she was talking to herself.

He had gone upstairs to tell her about his phone call with the local police, but the conversation fell short when it appeared she was trying to get rid of him. The kid appeared to be telling the truth. He had no prior arrests, and he showed them the hundred dollar bill. It wasn't necessarily evidence, but it did collaborate his story. They showed him a few pictures sent to them from the NYPD, but nothing was picked out. Either he was protecting someone, or he really didn't recognize anyone. Jax had to agree with the cops. In this case, more than likely, even the guy that gave him the money was uninvolved. They knew how to cover their tracks.

The bigger question right now? Was Brynn slipping from reality? He wouldn't blame her after all she'd been through. And now, she was trying to start over, and trouble was following her.

"Hey, Jax. I have some ideas to show you. You have a minute?"

Jax spun around to find Brynn standing there with sketches and pictures. "Sure, what do you have?"

She placed the plans for the upstairs bedroom in front of him, and he had to admit they were great. "I like it."

"Do you think we'll be able to find bathroom fixtures that will fit the décor?"

"Yeah. That'll be no problem."

"Great. Jax?"

He'd moved back to staining the woodwork. "Yeah?"

"Do you believe in ghosts?"

He stopped what he was doing. "I don't know. I suppose it's possible. Why are you asking?"

"What if I tell you, I think this place has one?"

"Are you telling me you believe in ghosts?"

"Not ghosts, really, just one."

"Does this have anything to do with why you're talking to yourself?"

"Would you be quiet?" she asked impatiently.

"You're the one that came in here and asked the questions."

"Not you, Jax. I guess there's only one way to break this to you. Sebastian Morgan, meet Jaxson Maddox."

Jax tightened his grip on the can of stain he held. What the hell? The first woman he'd actually had feelings for, and it was turning out she was a nutcase. And then…he appeared. Jax dropped the stain at his feet. He couldn't believe what he was seeing. An image of a man was fading in and out, and moving in his direction with an outreached hand. He stepped back.

"Don't be frightened, Jax. Sebastian's a good man."

He looked at Brynn in disbelief. And then reason snapped back into his head and he grabbed her arm, pulling her toward him. His eyes searched the room in all directions. "Whoever is doing this, I'll find you. You're not going to get near her with this made up bullshit."

Brynn turned toward him and clasped his hand. "It's not made up. Look at him, and then look at this picture."

He took the picture from her hand, studied it, then

looked at the image in front of him. "Anyone could do this sort of thing with the technology we have today. They're trying to get close."

She hadn't thought of this angle, but she knew this was the real Mr. Morgan. "Talk to him, Sebastian."

"It's true, sir, I am a ghost. I only just learned of this myself."

Jax shook his head. This couldn't be happening.

"Do you need to sit? I know this is shocking. I went through this myself. But Sebastian thought, considering the circumstances, we should let you in on it."

"Let me in on what?"

"We are in search of what these hooligans want. At this time, we don't know what that is, but we're going to find it. And you, kind sir, are welcome to join our hunt."

"You've got to be kidding." Jax leaned forward, putting his head in his hands.

"Does he have a case of the vapors, my dear?"

"I'm not sure. Jax?"

His head popped up. "No. I don't have the *vapors*."

Sebastian moved in closer. "He's looking a bit green about the gills."

"It's not every day a person meets a ghost, Sebastian."

"Would you two mind? This is a little hard to take."

Brynn kneeled in front of him. "I know, and I'm sorry. I didn't know how else to tell you. You would never have believed me. And you keep catching me talking to myself. Well, not myself really, but I'm sure that's how it looked."

"Brynn, you're babbling, dear."

She stole a glance over her shoulder at Sebastian. "I am, aren't I?" She turned back to Jax. "Are you okay with this?"

Jax laughed. "I've been introduced to a man that lived over a century ago, and you ask me if I'm okay with this?"

Yeah, he had her there.

Chapter Twenty-Three

"There's no need to get testy, sir. She is only worried about your condition. I believe him well. His color is returning."

"Would you quit staring at me?" Jax stood and put distance between him and the inquiring ghost. "Brynn, how do you know this isn't some sort of trick?"

"Our talks. No one could know the things he's told me."

"Like?"

He wanted examples. Okay. "Like the key to the trunk. Do you remember me telling you Sebastian told me where it was? He did."

"And I've been a champion for your cause, Mr. Maddox," Sebastian chimed in.

He shot him a look and then settled on Brynn. "What's he talking about?"

"Nothing."

"Poppycock. Nothing, she says." He repeated with sarcasm. "I've encouraged the lady to seek your protection, among other things."

"Other things?" He tried to cover the clipped tone in his voice, but his patience was running thin.

"I did suggest she was of marriageable age. However, I cannot condone your residence here until after the ceremony."

"Brynn, what the hell is he talking about?"

"A bunch of nonsense. Sebastian, could you leave us now, so I can talk to Jax?"

"You're risking your reputation without the company of a chaperone."

"Is he the one filling your head with dangers to your reputation?" His eyes seared into Sebastian's.

She placed a hand on his arm. "Jax, no. That's all me. Listen, he's one of the good guys. I've offered to help him find Helena."

"This is insane. I have a security company coming here in less than an hour. How do I explain the alarm being tripped by a ghost?"

"I'm not a solid mass. I'm not likely to trigger your alarm."

"He's still here, Brynn." Jax turned away from her and ran a hand through his hair.

"Sebastian, please, I need to talk to Jax alone."

He nodded curtly. "I understand. A lover's spat should not be witnessed by the masses. Carry on. I will be in my chambers tending to our plans."

"What is he talking about? Brynn, a ghost? How am I supposed to believe this? And every time I turn around is he going to be hovering?"

"He doesn't really hover. He floats a bit above the ground."

Jax raised an eyebrow. "I can't believe I'm having this conversation. What if I need to talk to you privately? He's just going to materialize wherever, or whenever, he wants? And the guys…how am I going to explain all the noises?"

"I know this is a shock. You'll need some time to process this, but Sebastian is real, and he's offered to help."

"I don't need his help. I'm perfectly capable of taking care of you without his help."

"First off, no one needs to take care of me." Brynn copped a bit of an attitude. "Secondly, Sebastian is able to move around here without anyone knowing he's here. He's found he can manifest to anyone he chooses. That could be a huge advantage. He's coming up with a plan," she added.

"He is, is he? Nice. How did I get replaced by the phantom of the shipyard?"

"Your feelings are hurt?"

He raised his voice, something he rarely did. "Yeah, Brynn, a little. I want to be your hero, not some vapor passing through."

Her face softened. "You have been my hero."

He reached out and pulled her into his arms, kissing the top of her head. "So, you want me to be friends with Casper?"

Sebastian floated in. "Why does everyone insist on calling me Casper? Is Sebastian so hard to remember?"

****

A short twenty minutes later, Jax was expected to act like everything was normal when the security crew entered. He, now, understood what Brynn had been going through. Sebastian was following them from room to room, looking over shoulders, and inspecting equipment. He was waiting for one of the workman to notice a component sailing across the room. The crew was there for hours, and eventually Sebastian lost interest and moved on to where ghosts go to when they aren't being a pain in the ass.

At least, Mike and his crew were elsewhere today. He wasn't sure how his old friend would take to a poltergeist.

The alarm was installed, checked, and instructions given. Now, it was time for them to leave. "Brynn, are you ready to go?"

Brynn entered the rotunda where Jax waited, followed by Sebastian. Her coat hung over her arm, and her briefcase was hanging in the air next to Sebastian. "Let me know what you think of those sketches. I'll be ordering furniture this week."

"Great. The return of Casanova."

"What's he talking about, my dear?"

"He doesn't care for the furniture salesman. He thinks he's a lady's man."

Anger flashed across Sebastian's face. "Then, I do not approve of him either. My former partner was of that type, and now my wife is gone." The disdain was in every syllable he uttered. "Do not take this lightly. If Mr. Maddox does not trust this man, you should heed his warning."

Maybe this ghost wasn't half bad after all. Jax was in a war with himself to speak or remain silent. He chose silence.

"Mr. Shuller is harmless, Sebastian. He only has a high opinion of himself."

"I cannot promise I will not scare him out of my home."

Brynn rolled her eyes. "We'll see you tomorrow."

"Good evening," he responded. "And it has been nice making your acquaintance, Mr. Maddox."

Jax nodded. What did you say to a ghost?

Chapter Twenty-Four

"I think we should use that gift certificate." Jax announced, while settling on her couch.

She hung up her coat. "I thought that was a bad idea."

"Well, with the watchful eye of Sebastian Morgan at the castle, maybe we can use this to our advantage. I'd wager a bet they already know about the castle. If we're out of the way, they might take the opportunity to make their move, and Sebastian can watch them. Maybe find out who they are, and what they're looking for."

"When would you want to do this? The movers are bringing my things tomorrow. What if what they're looking for is in there? We'd just be handing it over. And it's going to be a busy day with Brad coming to discuss furniture."

"It's Brad now?"

"You and I are friends, remember? You're dangerously close to crossing a line."

He grumbled something under his breath, then changed the subject. "Okay, so we'll pass it by Sebastian first. See if he thinks he can stop them if they have a hold of evidence."

"See?" She smiled. "It's not so hard to believe in ghosts."

****

Brynn arose the following day to sunshine sparkling on the snow-covered ground. The movers were coming today, and her excitement grew. She hadn't been excited about much since Nate died. Not even the purchase of the castle, really, because he was absent from that momentous occasion. But, today, her things would be around her, and she had to admit, that gave her comfort. And she'd be able to go through the box of Nate's from his police locker. There were a couple of other boxes that had odds and ends belonging to him, but she couldn't think of anything that might be evidence against Apollo Banks and his gang.

"Little lady, you're moving truck is here!" Mike shouted to her from below.

She turned to Sebastian. "You promise to behave yourself?"

"On my honor. I am only hoping your furniture isn't too dreadful." A sigh escaped his lips, and Brynn laughed.

"I told you it's my bed, a chair, a lamp, and some boxes. Brad will be coming this afternoon."

"Ah, yes, Casanova."

"Don't you start, or I won't let you help pick out the furniture."

Sebastian mimicked zipping his lip, and she grinned. Nate would have never believed this. "Stay up here, out of the way. It shouldn't take long."

Brynn greeted the movers and showed them the way to her temporary living space. She was surprised Jax hadn't made an appearance but was soon too busy to notice. They were gone in less than an hour, and she was left with the aftermath. Her focus strayed to the stack of boxes in the corner. Could there be something in there that would nail Apollo?

"Brynn?"

Startled, she spun around to find Jax standing in the doorway. "You scared me."

"Sorry. You need any help?"

"No, I'm good. The guys put the bed together. I just have to find the linens." Was it her imagination, or had he been avoiding her all morning? "Is something bothering you?"

"Not anything I can put my finger on." He glanced around the room before saying, "I'm going to get back to work. See you later."

That was some odd behavior. Maybe he decided a widow with a ghost was too much trouble. Who could blame him?

"You're residing in here?"

Brynn wasn't sure she'd ever get used to Sebastian's sudden appearances. "For a little while." Her mind was still preoccupied with the way Jax had acted toward her.

"You do realize this was my dining room?" Sebastian walked the perimeter of the room. "All the wood in this room was imported."

Brynn ran a hand over the woodwork. The intricate carving was throughout the room. "I've never seen anything like the artistry in this room. The plaster moldings are fantastic."

"It should be. It cost me a pretty penny." He moved over to the fireplace, also carved in wood. He glanced around the room. "I guess it is in need of repairs."

Brynn smile inwardly, not allowing the triumph to show. "I want to someday serve fine dinners in here to my guests."

"So, you do not plan to make it a bedroom?"

She sighed. It was time to break the news to him, and she wasn't sure how he was going to take it. "My plan is to make this into a bed & breakfast." There, she said it. It wasn't like he could do anything about it. She had purchased the castle fair and square. Then reality hit. He could do something…haunt the place. She had to convince him.

"You intend on turning my home into a boarding house?"

The disapproval was most definitely in his voice. "Not a boarding house, but a bed and breakfast."

"It would seem of very little difference to me. I'm sorry I can't allow it. I won't have strangers parading through my house."

Time for the convincing. "Sebastian, wouldn't you love to have this place alive again? Children laughing in its hallways, people sitting at the table eating meals together, gathering in the living room, walking the grounds…" He made no comment, so she continued. "I want to make Sebastian's Castle beautiful again. And I want people to enjoy that beauty."

He remained silent, pivoting slowly around the room, hands behind his back. "It might not be distasteful if done the proper way."

"What do you have in mind?"

"This year you speak of…2016? If the style is indicative of your bed, I would prefer we use furniture already on the grounds."

"You mean the furniture in the attic?"

"There is a storage area in the carriage house where many of the original pieces were carried off. Some were sold, even though the deed states the furniture was to stay with the castle. Of course, not everyone heeds an old man's will."

When she and Nate inspected the grounds, she only had eyes for the castle. Excitement bubbled up. "I've never been to the carriage house."

"It would seem we have a great deal of work to do, my dear, if we're to turn this into the show place it once was."

"Thank you, Sebastian, for helping make my dream come true. And my husband's."

He nodded with little expression, but Brynn had gotten to know him. He appeared gruff, but he was one of those teddy bear types. Never would she believe he had anything to do with his wife's disappearance.

"As I've said, you remind me of my Helena. As I told her, every princess needs a castle…and a prince."

"Brynn, did you call me?" Jax poked his head into the door.

"No, she did not, but I believe fate did." Sebastian's eyebrow raised when he looked in her direction.

Chapter Twenty-Five

Jax was preoccupied all day, barely saying two words to her. Brad Shuller had taken a tour of the castle, and they briefly discussed colors and styles. He was the perfect gentleman today. She knew what Jax thought of him, but she couldn't imagine that was the problem. At least, she hoped not. She made it perfectly clear that friendship was all she was interested in, and now, being here, and knowing the amount of work to be done…well, she couldn't focus on anything, or anyone else. She enjoyed his company, and that was that.

He had packed up his tools, and asked her if she remembered how to set the alarm, but seemed perfectly satisfied when she said she did. And that was out of character for him.

Night had descended quickly. Her day flew by collecting her things, and Romeo, from the inn. She wouldn't say it aloud, but she missed that room with its warm fireplace and comforting colors. She, now, sat cross-legged on her bed trying to distract herself with the catalogs Brad had left.

Brynn had to admit she was a little creeped out here. There was a small light plugged into an outlet in the rotunda, but it didn't give off much light. The long hallway was dark and quiet. Romeo had left her, exploring his new surroundings with his tail happily swinging in the air. A light illuminated her room. Her stomach grumbled for a piece of the leftover pizza she had ordered earlier, but she wasn't highly motivated to move from this spot.

From somewhere above, Romeo screamed, than hissed. She jumped from her bed and reached for her phone, ready to call the police. She relaxed when Sebastian's complaining drew closer.

"Who brought that foul rodent hunter in here?" he grumbled.

"That's Romeo. My cat."

"Well, he's going to have to go. Animals are not permitted in the castle."

"Whose rule is that?" She attempted to stifle a giggle.

"Mine. I just instated it."

"Romeo is staying. We're a package deal. Besides, he's a good hunter." Brynn sat back down on her bed, relaxing with Sebastian's company.

"My dear, you look like you've seen a ghost." He chuckled. "I guess you have, haven't you? Is my company distressing you?"

"No. Not at all. It's my first night here, and I guess I'm a little nervous. It's a little creepy here at night."

"Well, let's look at this logically, shall we? You do not have to worry about it being haunted, because you already know that it is. There's no reason to worry about the ghost, because he's quite fond of you, I assure you."

She smiled at that. "It's not you that I'm worrying about. I'm waiting for Banks and his gang to make a move. I'm a bit of a sitting duck."

"I have a few tricks up my sleeve if that should happen. Have you searched your husband's things?"

"Not yet."

"Grab the box, my dear, and let's see what we find." Brynn hesitated. "Situations, most generally, do not take care of themselves. To be prepared you must be well informed."

"You're right. I need to be on the offensive."

"Yes, my dear, whatever that means. Grab the box. Is this the one?"

She nodded. Across the side, written in black marker, was *Nate's things*. She lifted the box and laid it on the bed. Her hands shook. This was all that was physically left of her husband, his things. Yes, she had her precious memories, but she couldn't hug those close to her.

"You are not alone, Brynn. I am right here." It was the first time Sebastian had used her name. She looked over her shoulder to see him standing there. "I know the feelings you are having, but you can do this. Remember why you're doing this."

"I'm just not ready. The wounds are raw." She stared at the box, her hands resting on top.

"You are ready. You must be ahead of those who murdered him."

Brynn grabbed the tape and pulled. Now, all she had to do was look inside. Sitting on top, neatly folded, was the flag she had carefully packed. His Medal of Honor rested beside it. She closed her eyes briefly, swallowed back the emotion, and gently placed them aside. She rummaged through the rest and found a few baseball hats, a box of golf balls, the trophy his shift had won for bowling the year before. Nothing earth-shattering, and certainly nothing anyone would kill for. "There's nothing in here."

"Is that the only box?" Sebastian pushed.

She shook her head and grabbed another. Lowering herself on the bed, she ripped off the tape. "This is the box from his locker at the police department." One by one, she emptied the contents. A razor, shaving cream, deodorant, soap, shampoo… She stopped. In her hand was a photo taken of her and Nate one summer day at the park. She placed it face down on the bed beside her. She knew if she looked at it, her heart would sink even lower. Then, she lifted an old pair of court shoes from the box. "I'm surprised to find these in here. He hated them."

Sebastian moved closer but said nothing. Perplexed, she moved on, laying them on the bed next to the other things. Next, she pulled out a t-shirt and shorts. "He and the guys liked to play basketball after their shift," she explained. She peered in the box. "That's it."

"What about the other box?"

"That has some of his clothes I packed. I couldn't give them all away."

"I understand very well, my dear. The ball dress in the trunk…that was my Helena's favorite dress. She wore it for our marriage ceremony. I couldn't give it to strangers."

Going through his things gave her a heavy heart. She lifted the shoes to put them back in the box, and something fell out. "What's this?"

Sebastian leaned forward, inspecting it closely. "Never saw anything like it in all my days."

"I know what it is. I don't know why it was in Nate's shoe."

"What is it then?"

"A memory stick for computers. But why would it be…" She stopped. "This had to be what they were looking for. She jumped from the bed to retrieve his computer.

"What are you searching for?" Sebastian spun around keeping her in eyeshot.

"I'm looking for Nate's computer. This little thing holds memory…data…what they're after might be on that stick." She was both excited and fearful, then it occurred to her. "Nate's computer is gone. Now that I think about it, I don't remember packing it away, or even seeing it."

"When was the last you saw it? Was it before, or after, he was laid to rest?"

"Before. I remember him sitting on our bed, working on something. Where could it have gone?" Panic rose in the form of her shaky voice.

"Maybe you should contact his superiors at the police department."

Her reaction was to grab her phone, but that's as far as it went. Her instinct was telling her something different. "I don't know who I can trust. How do I know that someone in the department didn't sell him out, or leak he was undercover?"

"I can tell you who you can trust. Me. And that contractor of yours. The one that would move mountains for you to get to the other side."

"I don't want to endanger anyone."

"Have you forgotten I'm already dead?"

"No, I have not forgotten. I can't drag Jax into this." It was becoming second nature to talk to a ghost.

"You must learn to trust again. He cares for you very much. Call him, and we'll form a plan of action."

"But, it's late. I don't want to bother him."

"Land's sake, girl, it's only nine. He can't be that boring. Call him. Get him over here, so we can go over the logistics."

Should she? Or would that be opening a new can of worms?

Chapter Twenty-Six

"Jax, it's Brynn. Did I wake you?" She bit down on her lip.

"A little bit early for that. What can I do for you?"

He was sounding strangely formal. She hesitated. Maybe this wasn't the right thing to do. If she dragged him into this, there would be no turning back. He could very possibly be in danger.

"Brynn?"

"Yeah. I'm here. I'm trying to decide if I should drag you into this."

"What? What's wrong?" The urgency in his voice indicated he cared. There was no hiding that.

She couldn't lead him on, but Sebastian was right. She trusted him. "I went through Nate's things," she blurted.

"I'm sure that was hard. Did you find anything?"

"Sebastian thought I should call you. I thought about calling the detective in New York, but…"

"But?" Jax urged.

"How do I know they didn't sell Nate out? It would be the same as handing it over to Banks."

"Hand what over? You think someone in the NYPD is involved?"

"There's no real reason to believe that, just a feeling. I know not all cops are good. It's part of life—good and bad. When there's a bunch of money involved, well, it makes good people do stupid things."

"What can I do to help?"

"I may have found something."

"I'll be right over. I'll ring your cell when I get there."

She didn't have a chance to say goodbye before he hung up.

"He's on his way?"

"Yeah. Sebastian, I hope I didn't make a huge mistake by calling him. If anything happens to him, because of me…"

****

Jax really tried to play it cool with her today. He thought maybe she would see having him around wasn't a bad thing and approach him. But it hadn't happened. She kept busy most of the day and never searched him out. And now, the phone call. Whatever it was, she was shook up, and playing it cool was out the window. She asked him for help. That's all he needed to know.

On the drive to the castle, he wondered how he had fallen so quickly for this damsel in distress. Was that why? She was wounded, and he needed to fix her? Somehow he didn't believe that. He thought about nothing, but her. It didn't matter if she was in the next room or across town.

He drove up the lane a little faster than normal. The old light posts that lined the short road to the castle remained dark. Another thing on the *to-do* list. They would update the lights for security.

Jax stopped, threw the truck in park, and jumped out—almost in one fluid motion. "Damn!" He retrieved his cell from his pocket and dialed her number, while waiting at the door. He wanted her to be cautious, and not assume anything.

She picked up. "I'm here." The door opened. The phone was still at his ear.

Brynn looked from side to side, searching…but, what, or who, was she looking for? "Come on in." She secured the lock behind him.

Jax crossed the threshold to find Sebastian a few feet away in the hallway. His image was strong, not fading in and out like normal. "Who's going to tell me what's wrong?"

"Come back to the dining room. I don't have furniture anywhere else." She led Jax back to her makeshift bedroom. Under different circumstances he would have been more aware, but not now. Now, he was worried about whatever had developed.

Sebastian stood against the wall looking grave. Another reason to worry. This guy never shut up. "Well?"

She lowered herself on the bed and motioned for him to sit in the chair across from her. She inhaled a deep breath. "I went through Nate's things, and I found this." She held out her open hand. A memory stick rested in her palm.

"What's on it?" Whatever it was, it couldn't be good with the look on their faces.

"I don't know yet. I went to get Nate's computer and realized it's missing."

"So, you still have yours, right?"

"I do, but… I realized Nate's computer is gone. I don't remember seeing it after he died."

"Load that in to your computer, and see what's on it. Maybe there's information on it that could end this."

"I'm afraid to know what's on it. I shouldn't have called you. Whatever it is could put you in danger too."

Jax leaned toward her. "I don't care about that. I'll do whatever it takes to help you. I've told you that before."

"But before we were talking about renovating a castle, not going after dangerous men who could have murdered my husband."

Sebastian remained quiet until that moment. "Tell him where you found the hardware, Brynn."

"It was in a pair of shoes he hated. They were retrieved from his locker after he…died."

"And you think this might be significant?"

"I don't know. As soon as I saw the shoes, alarm bells went off. I thought he'd thrown them out. He was constantly complaining how uncomfortable they were. So, when I saw them it didn't make sense."

"What are you thinking?"

"That maybe he knew I'd question why he still had those shoes and look a little deeper."

"Okay, so let's look a little deeper. Get your computer."

She paled.

"Brynn, you can do this. I'm right here with you." He glanced over at Sebastian. "We're both here. I bet this gang leader doesn't have a ghost on his side?"

A hint of a smile crossed Brynn's face.

"I can assure you, any ghost helping that hoodlum would have no brains. I, dear lady, have a proven track record of my intelligence."

Brynn rubbed her hands together, obviously attempting to quiet the anxiety. She reached over into her nightstand and pulled out her computer. She flipped it open and pushed the power button. Jax moved to the bed, sitting behind her. Sebastian held vigil against the wall. It seemed like forever while the computer loaded. Jax took the memory stick from her hand and inserted it into the port. The oxygen seemed to be sucked from the room, as hearts pounded harder in wait.

There was one file that appeared. "Click on it, Brynn. It's okay." He really hoped he wasn't leading her astray.

It was a note addressed to Brynn.

Brynn,

I hate to be cliché and say if you're reading this I'm gone, but unfortunately that's probably the case. I don't have a good feeling about tonight's bust. I've hidden my computer with all the evidence they'll need to nail Apollo Banks and put him away for a long, long time. Do not, and I repeat, do not hand it over to my precinct. Better yet, when you find the computer contact the FBI.

I know you're smart, Brynn. No one would think to look in a pair of court shoes, but I knew you would. I hate those shoes. I was hoping you'd remember that. I wish I could tell you who you could trust, but I have no idea if corrupt cops are involved. Remember, these people will stop at nothing to keep their business going. Find the computer. Remember our dream, and it will lead you.

I have loved you with every breath I've taken, and I will love you in eternity. Be happy. That's all I've ever wanted for you.

All my love,

Nate

Brynn's back was to Jax, but he saw her shoulders

shake with grief. He wasn't going to let her go through this alone. No, he was going to be the one she could trust.

Chapter Twenty-Seven

Brynn rubbed at the moisture on her face. She couldn't fall apart. Nate would want her to be strong, to figure out the puzzle, and finish what he started. She stood. "I'm all right."

"If you need a moment alone to compose yourself, Mr. Maddox and I will understand."

She faced them both. "I'm fine. I'll deal with the emotions later. Right now, I have to find that computer before they find me first."

"I don't like this. If you do this, you're going to be putting yourself in a hell of a place. No. There has to be another way."

"And what would that be? Without knowing what Nate had on them, there is no other way. I have to find that computer before they do." She reread the note. "He said to 'remember our dream.'" The only dream they talked about was this castle. What could he possibly be referring to?

"We need to show the note to the authorities, Brynn."

"I brought you here, because I trust you. Don't betray that trust. I can't go to the police. Nate said as much."

"But you need protected."

"We'll protect her, my dear boy." Sebastian spoke from the corner. "But maybe there's something you'd like to share about your background?"

What are you talking about?" Jax asked.

Great. That's all she needed—her only friend, next to a ghost, with something to hide. "What do you know, Sebastian?" She glanced over to where Jax stood, the nerves coursing through her body at an all new high.

"I have observed Mr. Maddox when he thought an intruder was in the castle. He carries himself like someone with a background in police work."

"So, maybe I'm just careful."

One by one, Brynn's muscles released the tension she held, waiting for his answer. There was no hidden background. Jax had told her his former career. She looked with admiration at the man standing there. Little by little, day by day, she realized her feelings for him involved much more than gratitude.

"Maybe you should tell him, Jax," Brynn suggested.

"Yeah. Okay. Before I was a general contractor, I was in the Military Police Corps."

"You never mentioned that tidbit." Sebastian faded in and out, indicating his distress.

"It never came up. Do you have something against cops?"

"My last encounter with the police force was less than pleasurable. In my day, they were not without corruption. It would seem, not much has changed in this century. At any rate, I have never heard of the Military Police Corps, but I shall assume you know how to handle a weapon, and a crisis?"

"Is this a job interview, Sebastian?"

Sebastian directed his next comment to Brynn. "I am lifting my ban of Mr. Maddox living in residence. I believe it a necessity."

"Really, I don't think…"

"It's a very good idea, my dear. I believe you to be a smart woman, but there's power in numbers. Wouldn't you say, Mr. Maddox?"

"I'd have to agree, Brynn."

Brynn hesitated. Jax living in the castle would put her in close proximity to him every single hour of the day. Her feelings for him were spiraling out of control. She didn't want to fall in love with him, but she couldn't use *that* for her argument. "I wanted a new start. I don't want to be known as the town hussy."

"I will be here to chaperone," Sebastian added.

Brynn rolled her eyes and lowered herself to the bed.

"My truck outside might deter any move they were planning, knowing you aren't alone. I would expect them to have to regroup."

"And when they do?" Her heart sped up at the thought.

"We have to locate this computer. Once we have that, and we know what's on it, we can contact the FBI and allow them to greet them at the door."

"How are we going to find the computer?"

"Well, Brynn, that ball's in your court. I believe you already know. We just have to pull the memory out of you." He grabbed his coat from the chair.

"Are you leaving?" Did she sound too desperate? The thought of him going petrified her on so many levels. She worried about his safety, of course, but when he was with her she felt whole, and that scared her the most. Nate was slipping away.

"I'm going home to pick up some clothes. Why

don't you come with me?"

"I'll be fine. You go ahead."

He glanced at Sebastian.

"I will watch over her. I can be quite scary when I need to be."

He nodded. "I won't be gone long." He looked to Brynn. "Set the alarm, and don't answer the door without knowing it's me. Got it?"

"Yeah. Got it. And Jax?" He stopped and turned. "Thanks for doing this."

He winked and was out the door. And she was left with the aftermath of that simple gesture.

****

"How am I ever going to find this computer?" She sighed loudly.

Sebastian paced the floor in front of her, his index finger resting on his chin as he walked to and fro.

"Will you stop pacing?" Her frazzled nerves couldn't handle much more.

"I know I'm being remiss with something."

Brynn gathered everything in the box, except the picture. She leaned it against the lamp on her nightstand. Sebastian moved closer, looking at the picture.

"This is your husband?"

She nodded. "It was taken the summer before he died."

"I've seen him before." He continued to gaze at the picture.

"Who? Nate? How would you see him? Oh, wait, when we came to tour the castle?"

Sebastian turned away from the picture and said to Brynn, "I don't remember you. Only him. You accompanied him?"

"Yes. It was me, Nate, and the realtor." Why did she expect something bad to come from this conversation?

"Brynn, I cannot recall what he did while he was here, but he was alone. Sometimes, many times, I lost interest in the trespassers and went elsewhere. My frame of mind wasn't the best in those days. Why do you suppose he was here?"

Her nerve endings crawled across her skin. The wind rattled the windows, making the attempt to exude confidence in front of the ghost more difficult. She walked to the front window, off the rotunda, and peered out. The snowstorm predicted last week had arrived. She hadn't bothered to keep up on the reports with more pressing issues on her mind. Jax had been gone awhile. She hoped he was safe. Not only did she have to worry about him getting caught up with gang members but keeping his truck on the road.

"You're worried about him?" Sebastian observed.

"It doesn't mean what you're implying."

"What am I implying?" He feigned surprise.

"I would be worried about any friend out in this weather." She paced back to the front door. A vibrating sound came from down the hall—the carriage entrance. Her eyes widened. She looked to Sebastian standing next to her. He placed his index finger to his mouth, and pointed for her to retreat back down the hallway. She silently waited in her makeshift bedroom with her cell gripped tightly in her hand. Had they found her?

Chapter Twenty-Eight

Jax rummaged through his garage in search of his old Army cot. Brynn was short on furniture, and sleeping on an old, dirty, cold floor didn't appeal to him. He'd set up camp in what would be her rooms. If he had a hard time sleeping, as he thought he would with her close proximity, he could get some work in while she slept.

He threw his duffel bag into the back seat, and the cot in the bed of the truck. Huge, heavy snowflakes were falling from the sky, sometimes sideways with the wind that was kicking up. A black SUV drove by slowly. He watched the taillights disappear in the distance. The roads were fast becoming dangerous, and he imagined anyone out tonight would be driving slowly. However, it was his nature to be suspicious.

Jax climbed into the warmth of his truck and shifted it in four-wheel drive. He glanced at the clock on the dash. He'd been gone longer than he thought. Remembering where he stashed the cot had been an issue. He pulled to a four way stop, and the black SUV sat at the side of the road. There were no hazard lights blinking, just the brake lights illuminating the snow. The inside of the car was completely dark. There was no way Jax was stopping. It was too remote, and with this weather, he could be asking for trouble. He slowly made his way around the vehicle. He made an attempt to see in the driver's side, but the windows were tinted, and the snow fell too heavily. His instincts were on high alert. The vehicle just didn't fit for Mystic.

Watching the road and keeping an eye behind him, he put some distance between him and the SUV. Just when his muscles relaxed, he noticed headlights moving at the same pace as he was. Almost sure he was being tailed, he turned down a side street. He wasn't surprised to see the lights round the corner. His advantage was knowledge of the area. If these guys were from New York, they had a limited familiarity of these roads. Losing the tail was a priority, and getting back to Brynn a must. He prayed they were trying to find her through him and not trying to delay him.

Jax chose a confusing allotment to lose the tail. The roads looped around and all looked similar. If a person was from out of town, they'd get mixed up fast. He exited out the back of the allotment, with no sign of the SUV. Satisfied, he had to get back to Brynn. He had an awful feeling he was being delayed.

The windshield wipers ran at full speed, and the wind blew his truck around. Holding the wheel with both hands, he neared the entrance to Sebastian's castle. Was that a truck up ahead? He drew closer to find a dark-colored, full sized pick-up outside the entrance. The adrenaline pumped through his veins. He pulled into the drive, and the truck sped off. Yeah, this wasn't good.

There was no time to worry about license plates or descriptions. He pushed down on the accelerator and made his way to the carriage entrance. Nothing appeared out of the ordinary at first glance. He pounded on the door, muttered an expletive, and pulled out his phone. It was ringing too many times. The thought crossed his mind to kick in the door, but Brynn answered her phone. "Let me in," he ordered. He didn't know who was inside with her. He didn't care. Jax grabbed the gun from his holster, cocked it, and held it behind his back, ready to use it. His training kicked in, and he was aware of everything around him. The door opened. Was it his imagination, or did she look pale?

He moved passed her, while she shut the door. The sliding of the bolt lock echoed behind him. "Everything okay? Where's Sebastian?"

"We had a little incident, but we're safe now."

"Damn it! I knew it! What happened?"

"I was watching out the front window, waiting for you to come down the lane. We heard a noise coming from here. Sebastian ordered me back to my room, so I don't really know what happened, except he scared whoever it was, and they took off."

Jax's instinct was to go out and check around the grounds, especially since a truck took off right before he got in here. They may have ditched someone, and they could be hiding close by. He had to resist the urge, knowing he could be ambushed. This damn weather didn't help either. "Do you have any idea where Sebastian went off to?"

"I don't. You said you knew something happened. How?"

"I was tailed by a black SUV. I had to take the time to lose them. I had a feeling I was being held up. They know you're here, Brynn." He stormed off toward the rotunda. "Sebastian! Where the hell are you?"

He appeared almost immediately. "I was doing a bit of reconnaissance work. You needn't yell."

Jax ignored the statement. “Did you see anyone?”

“Not during my circuit around the castle.”

“I really don’t have time for your cryptic sentences.”

“There’s no need to panic. I scared the hoodlum away. He bolted through the snow like a scared rabbit.” Sebastian chuckled and seemed pleased with his handling of the situation.

“Okay, from the top.” Jax’s patience was long gone.

Sebastian asked Brynn, “Did you tell him about the noise? I don’t want to be redundant.”

“Just tell the story,” Jax grumbled through gritted teeth.

“A noise sounded from this direction. I sent Brynn back to the dining room. I shut off the alarm and opened the door.”

“You opened the door to murderers?” Jax couldn’t believe his ears.

“Well, yes. For you, that may have not been a wise move, but one look at me…or through me, as the case would be…and he was off and running. I don’t believe his feet touched the ground.”

Jax swiped a hand through his hair. He supposed that wasn’t a bad idea. He’d go back and tell his buddies the place was haunted. “Why did you shut off the alarm?” He didn’t want to think what would have happened if a scare from a ghost wouldn’t have sufficed.

“It was a judgment call. If the local police are involved, they will call the New York police. We were trying to avoid that, were we not?”

“Yeah.” He turned to Brynn, searching her face. He

would have never forgiven himself if anything would have happened to her. From here on in, until this was over, he would not leave her side. "You're not hurt?"

"No, Jax. I never saw anyone to get hurt. Sebastian handled it." She paused and looked toward her guard ghost. "Thank you. I don't know what I would have done without you here."

"You're very welcome, my dear girl. It would seem time is of the essence to find the commuter."

"Computer," Jax corrected.

"Of course. The computer. Considering the circumstances of this evening, I think I should share with you some information."

The ghost was holding out on them?

Chapter Twenty-Nine

Brynn held in her two cents and waited for Sebastian to share. Jax appeared two breaths away from a blow up. He was worried for her. She could see it when she opened the door…the look of panic. She knew it well. She couldn't allow herself to think about that. Her attention moved back to Sebastian as he spoke.

"Considering the safety concern for Brynn, and you too, of course, I will divulge information that no one else knew about the castle. Not even my Helena. There are secret tunnels below the mansion."

"I knew it!" She glanced at Jax, not even attempting to hide the smug smile.

"Yeah, but then, we were looking for a flesh and blood human, not someone who could walk through walls," Jax countered.

"True," she conceded. "Sebastian, why didn't you tell your wife about the passageways?"

"My relationship with my *former* partner was not amicable. I didn't trust him. The tunnels were put in place for an escape, or to remain hidden from any possible threat. I didn't inform Helena of their existence, simply to keep it secure." He looked to Jax. "You know how women can be? Clucking to their friends about this, or that."

Brynn glanced at Jax for his reaction to the

comment, before letting loose on the poltergeist. "That's a very sexist statement, Sebastian Morgan."

"Oh boy," Jax said just loud enough for her to hear him.

She ignored him. "I'm sure your wife was perfectly capable of keeping it a secret."

"Sexist statement? I suppose that's a conversation for another time. At the time, Helena had grown close to…"

Brynn's anger was snuffed by sympathy. She was well read on Sebastian's history. She knew the unsaid words. "You don't have to go into your personal life. I'm sure you had your reasons. Why tell us?"

"If these people attempt to gain entrance before we're ready, you'll have a place to hide while I scare the living daylights out of them."

"That's a very good idea. A safe zone. But I won't be leaving Brynn's side until this is over."

Sebastian nodded. "I would expect nothing less from you. Now, gather your flashlight, Miss Brynn, we're going on a tour."

Brynn did as suggested, gathering two from her makeshift bedroom. She returned and handed one to Jax. They stood in the rotunda. "Where to first?"

"The ladies' reception room." This small sized room was right off the rotunda in the front of the house. Brynn had tossed around how to use the space. The hand-carved fireplace was the focus of the room. "I had a door placed in this room, in case Helena needed a quick escape."

"How could she have ever used it, when she didn't know it existed?" Brynn still wrestled with the subject.

"It was not my intent to keep it from her, until her

loyalty seemed to wane." The sadness in his voiced effected Brynn. She knew that loss. At least, when Nate left this earth, she knew he loved her. She and Sebastian did share one thing in common. They both had unfinished business to handle regarding their spouses. At that moment, she knew she would help Sebastian find the truth.

"Do you want to guess where it is?"

Jax surveyed the room. The placement of a secret door wasn't obvious. "It's well hidden. Where?"

Sebastian motioned toward the hutch on the far interior wall. "Grab the back of it and pull forward as you would a door."

Jax did as instructed, and the hutch swung easily from the wall. "I have to admit, this is very cool." A smile spread across his face.

"There are steps going down. Shine your light to make sure they appear intact. I used the highest quality lumber around. I had great connections in the ship building business."

Jax lowered himself down first. If something was going to give, he wanted it to be to him. "It's safe, Brynn, careful…" He waited for her on a dirt floor below the castle, shining the light so she could see. From his right, Sebastian spoke, startling him. Would he ever get used to his sudden appearances?

"You will see a handle toward the bottom of the hutch. Grab it and pull it back in place."

No one would look at that piece of furniture and think it was moveable, let alone an entrance to a secret passage. When he first saw the piece sitting in the room his thoughts ran toward understanding. He would leave it here too, before he tried to move it.

Brynn waited below with Sebastian, asking if the design was his.

"Yes, my dear, it is my design. I loved dabbling in new ideas. My ships were full of new innovations."

"It's impressive, Sebastian," Jax chimed in. He shined the flashlight around. The passage was slightly narrower than a typical hallway, the floors were dirt, and the walls were constructed of the same cut marble as the outside of the structure. Hanging from the walls were simple wrought iron candle holders.

Sebastian made a sweeping motion, and in an instant the candles were burning brightly down the passageway. "How did you do that?" Brynn knew her mouth gaped open, but this was a worthy moment.

"I've picked up a thing or two in recent weeks. It's amazing what opened up for me when I realized I was a ghost. Are you ready for a look around?"

"Lead the way." Jax motioned for Brynn to go ahead of him. He was keeping a close eye on her, and it really did give her a warm feeling someone cared about her.

And she could really use that warm feeling down here. The place was freezing. "You're going to have to make this a quick tour, Sebastian. It's a little cold down here."

"Oh. I hadn't thought about that. I don't get cold. Okay. I'll take you up here, and we'll exit. At least, you will know two entrance points."

They followed the same passageway until it wound to the right. As soon as they rounded the corner the candles erupted into flames. "Oh, dear. I guess I overdid that a bit. Follow me right around here. Yes, there it is."

A wrought iron spiral staircase led somewhere above ground. "Where does this go?" Jax flashed his light up the steep staircase.

"This leads to the solarium, right off of the dining room. Miss Brynn's temporary quarters."

"The door's locked from above. We won't be able to get in that way."

"No worries, my girl. You forget who you're talking to."

Brynn was about to say something in return, but Sebastian was gone.

"After you," Jax said with a smile.

"What am I supposed to do when I get up there?"

"I suppose we'll figure it out. I'll be right behind you."

They reached the top, and Jax shined his light around her. He squeezed in close, sending shivers across her skin, that she attributed to the cold temperature. Jax spotted a handle and reached up, turning it. He slowly lifted it open. Brynn climbed through, followed by Jax. Sebastian waited by the open door leading to her bedroom.

"Right through here to the warmth." Sebastian bowed deeply.

Jax lowered the hatch back in place. If she didn't know it was there now, she would have never guessed. It blended in so well.

"Thank you, Sebastian, for sharing this with us. I feel safer knowing it's here."

"You're very welcome. Now, let's get down to the business of finding that commuter."

Chapter Thirty

"I need to get my things out of the truck and move it to the carriage house," Jax announced.

"No," Brynn blurted. "You can't go out there…the weather." She sounded a little too desperate, even to herself. The weather was the last thing she was worried about, even though the wind pounded against every upright object. "What if someone's out there?" Okay. She said it.

"I'll be fine."

"Yeah, famous last words. My husband said the same thing to me." She said it without thinking. Her face heated with embarrassment. "I mean…" What did she mean?

"No one would be standing around waiting in this weather."

"You're probably right. But leave the truck. There's no need to move it. They know I'm here."

"What about keeping the low profile?"

Brynn glanced across the room at Sebastian. He didn't appear to be paying attention. She said softly, "I don't care about that. I want you to come back safely. That's what I'm worried about."

Jax closed the distance between them. He pushed a lock of hair behind her ear. "Staying safe is my personal goal, because keeping you safe is my priority. I won't be long."

Brynn watched him pile on his coat, hat, and gloves. She followed him to the door. The cold wind blew in, taking her breath away as he exited. She had no windows at this entry to peer out, but she had ears, and one sign of trouble she was done. She'd hand them over whatever they wanted. Nate was gone, and she realized in this moment the feelings for Jaxson Maddox were not going to go away. She might not be ready to date anyone, but she would not let anything happen to him, because of her past.

Two beeps sounded, alerting her Jax had locked his truck. She threw open the door, and he rushed in with an old wooden cot and a duffel bag. Her eyes raised in question.

"Army issue. It's better than sleeping on the floor."

The guilt smacked her in the face. She hadn't thought of his sleeping arrangements. He was going to be uncomfortable on that old rickety thing. "You're doing so much for me. How am I ever going to repay you?"

"When this is all over I'm going to ask you out on a date, and you're going to go." He walked off toward the kitchen, leaving her standing in stunned silence.

"I believe I may have had a breakthrough."

Brynn leaped in surprise. "Sebastian, you have to quit doing that."

"I am sorry. Until you arrived, I believed I was a flesh and blood human. I'm still getting used to the idea myself. At any rate, I believe I may remember where I saw your Mr. Austin."

"Really? Where?" Her heart pounded. The idea of Nate keeping secrets from her…she didn't think that was the relationship they had.

"I believe I saw him entering the tunnels. I'm having difficulty remembering where. I didn't follow him, because really, there's not much down there to disturb. But I do believe he was carrying something."

Her blood thumped through her veins for a different reason. "Do you think it could have been the computer?"

Jax entered. "What's going on?"

"Sebastian remembers Nate going to the tunnels and carrying something with him."

"I cannot recall where he entered." Sebastian was fading in and out, a sure sign of his frustration.

"How many tunnels are below?" Jax went into cop mode. His demeanor changed right in front of her.

"They run the perimeter of the basement. Back in the day we had a swimming pool and bowling alleys down there." Sebastian proudly boasted. "This was quite the place."

"Funny, the realtor never showed me the basement."

"I'm afraid that might be my fault. I gave her quite the fright down there." He quickly added, "But it was never my intention."

"Let's get back to Nate and the computer." Jax reined in the conversation. "Can you think of a particular spot that might have had a good hiding area?"

Sebastian paced back and forth, arms crossed in front of him. "The rathskeller."

"What's a rathskeller?" Brynn knew the word, but not the meaning.

"It's a place where they served alcohol. Here, it would be like a home bar," Jax explained.

Brynn unsuccessfully attempted to hold in her

emotions, but she had to share. "When Nate and I talked about buying this place, he wanted to have a small restaurant that looked old world. I thought it was too big of an idea to start with, but we could add it to our list of dreams." She turned to Jax. "The note spoke of our dreams. Do you think?"

"It's a logical place to start. Do you want to wait until morning? It's late."

"I'll never be able to sleep wondering if it's down there. We have to find it first. I'll get my coat."

****

That left Sebastian and Jax. "How would he have found the tunnels? Doesn't make sense."

"I wondered that myself. There were no blueprints drawn, and I paid extra for the builder's silence. You don't think?"

"What?"

"I was cheated out of my money? Or perhaps, Mr. Austin found a map? There wasn't supposed to be a map." Sebastian disappeared, and as suddenly reappeared.

Jax needed Sebastian to guide them through. He couldn't stand by and allow him to evaporate in a panic. "He, most likely, stumbled across an entrance."

"I do suppose that's a valid possibility."

Brynn arrived, bundled in complete snowstorm gear. He couldn't resist. "The storm's outside."

"Funny. But when we get down there and you're whining like a girl, we'll see who's laughing. Are we ready?"

"Lead the way, Sebastian."

As they approached the stairs near the kitchen, Jax followed the ghost. *A ghost.* The real kicker was Jax thought of him as a friend. He'd protected Brynn, was part of their day, and now was helping them locate something that had nothing to do with him. Jax met quite a few bad characters in his days with the military police. He was willing to bet money Sebastian had done nothing to hurt his wife. Once Brynn was safe, he was going to do whatever he could to help Sebastian find closure.

They descended into the basement. Sebastian turned right. "What's the other way down here?" Jax wanted to know.

"Servants' quarters," he said, matter-of-factly.

They made another right and a wooden door opened in front of them. Again, candles illuminated the octagon-shaped room. All the furniture was gone, but Jax could imagine what the room might have looked like.

"This way. You'll have to use your lights." Sebastian directed. He led them down more steps into a room with a dirt floor. "This was the wine cellar. Over here." In front of their eyes, a floor to ceiling wine rack opened, revealing a small doorway.

Jax wondered how wine bottles would have stayed in place when the door was opened, but was sure Sebastian had it all figured out, and right now he had to concentrate on one thing—finding Nate's computer. The doorway was narrow, and he squeezed through without incident, followed by Brynn. The passageway they entered looked no different than what they'd seen previously.

He looked to Sebastian. "Any ideas where to start?"

"I'd say, right behind you."

Chapter Thirty-One

The blood left Brynn's face. There it was, right in front of her. Could the answers to all her questions be waiting on it? And was she ready for the answers? She leaned against the wall behind her.

Jax amazed her. He noticed right away her world was spinning. "Hey, there. Take a few deep breaths, Brynn. We're right here with you."

She nodded, unable to speak. Finding the computer was the center of her focus, and now they found it…she wondered if the answers were worth the pain. "I don't think I can do this."

Jax stood in front of her, face to face, with a tough expression. "Do you regret marrying a cop?" She didn't answer, and his voice grew louder. "Do you?"

"No."

"Doesn't sound like you mean it."

"Jax, what are you doing?" The tears filled her eyes.

"Do you regret marrying Nate Austin?"

"No!" The force of her words surprised her. "No." She repeated.

"You're a cop's wife. You're no shrinking violet. Every time Nate left the house you knew he might never come back. You had to be mentally tough to handle that. You stood at his funeral, followed the dream you shared, and all on your own. You're going to stop now? What's on that computer has the potential to put away the monsters that did this. Are you going to let them get away with this?"

Brynn swiped at the moisture on her face. He was right. This wasn't going to go away, and she wasn't going to go down without a fight. "You're right." She needed those words thrown in her face. "Thank you."

Jax squeezed her hand, before bending down to retrieve the computer. "Let's get out of here."

Within minutes they were back in her room. Jax opened the computer and pushed the button. "As I expected. No battery power left. Brynn, do you have the power cord to this?"

"No, but it's exactly like mine." She opened the bag that held her computer and handed him the power cord. He immediately plugged it in.

From behind Jax, Sebastian commented. "So, this is a commuter? An interesting invention."

"It's a computer," Jax corrected. "Here we go. It's loading." The password screen appeared. "Brynn, what's his password?"

A sick feeling passed through her. "I have no idea. I never asked."

Jax brushed a hand through his cropped hair and leaned his head back in frustration.

"Is there an issue?" Sebastian asked.

"Yeah. A little. A password must be entered to gain access. People set their own passwords. We have no way in. Brynn, do you have any good guesses?"

She suggested a few and all were denied. "Now what?" Brynn had prepared herself for the worst, and now another delay.

"I have a way in, but I need to get something from

my place."

"Jax, please don't go tonight."

Sebastian chimed in. "I think the lady has had much to deal with this day. Maybe a little rest is in order. I will leave you two to work out the details. I, myself, am not used to such excitement."

"You sleep?" Jax asked.

"I recharge, Mr. Maddox." With that, he disappeared.

"He's right. I'm frazzled. As much as I want to get to the bottom of this, I need a break."

"You got it. I'm a little tired myself. I'll just be a yell away."

He stood, and she fought the urge to grab him. "Jax, would you mind…um…staying in here…with me? I'm on edge with everything that's happened, and the wind's so loud…I guess I'm a little spooked."

Jax chuckled.

"What?" She shouldn't have asked him.

"You say you're spooked, and yet, you hang out with Casper. Speaking of, your chaperone isn't going to approve of me staying in here."

Her eyes were the first to sting, followed by her nose. She lowered her head, so he couldn't see the upcoming waterworks. "I'm being silly. You're right."

He sat beside her and slid his index finger under her chin. He lifted her eyes to his, forcing her to look at him. "You're not silly. You need to be aware that the friendly ghost might turn into an angry poltergeist. He's protective of you."

She had to admit she had a soft spot for Sebastian too. He was a good man…ghost…whatever, and she would help him the way he helped her. "I think he's loosened up his restrictions."

Jax stood. "I'll be right back."

"Where are you going?" Sleep. She needed to sleep. She was far too emotional.

"It's okay. I'm going to get the cot."

"No. If you're on that rickety piece of wood, I won't be able to sleep. You'll sleep here with me…and Romeo." The cat was already settled into the thick comforter.

His eyes widened. "Brynn, I don't think…"

She smiled. "It's a very good idea. We'll both be comfortable. We *are* adults, Jax."

"All right, you tuck yourself in. I'm going to check the locks and make sure the alarm is set. That should give you time to do…whatever females do before going to bed."

****

Jax checked both windows and doors, taking his time, and doing a lot of muttering. He'd sleep better on a rickety old cot. He should have told her no. Maybe, he still would. He could sleep in the chair. Fact was, he probably wasn't going to sleep well anyway. Jax didn't expect any unwelcome visitors due to the weather conditions, but he couldn't let his guard down.

Tomorrow was Saturday. There would be no crew here for the weekend. He would have called them off anyway. He watched the wind blow the snow sideways, past the window. There must be a foot of snow out there. And it was all blowing and drifting. Hopefully, what power they had didn't go off. There was no generator to back up the electric.

"It sure is coming down out there."

"Damn it, Sebastian. Do you want to make some

noise before you appear out of thin air?"

"Not really. It's much more fun this way."

"I'm staying in Brynn's room tonight. She asked me, so don't go turning all Freddy Krueger on me."

"Freddy Krueger?"

"Never mind. I get you're protective of her. I am too."

"She's understandably shaken. You will be honorable?"

"Of course. What do you take me for?"

"Then you have my blessing."

"I cannot believe I'm asking permission from an apparition."

"You respect my place in the castle, and maybe you care what I think?"

"I'd never admit it." Jax smirked into the darkness.

"You're a good man, Mr. Jaxson Maddox. I hope you make that young lady fall in love with you." With that, Sebastian disappeared as quickly as he arrived.

Chapter Thirty-Two

Brynn waited nervously for Jax's return. She flipped on the television that sat a few feet away, turning it to the weather station. There was no end to the snow anytime soon, or the wind. The storm had been upgraded to a blizzard. Her food supply wasn't the greatest. She had canned goods, a few things in the freezer, bottled water, wine, and junk food. Her lips pulled down into a frown.

"Why the sour look?" Jax asked from the doorway.

"It's been upgraded to a blizzard."

"Well, we'll just have to deal with it. The good news is we, most likely, won't get unexpected company. The bad news is I won't be able to go to my place to get what I need to crack the password."

"I'm afraid I don't have much of a food stock. We won't starve, but we're going to be eating a lot of soup. And I'm always stocked with junk food."

"Are they saying how long it's predicted to last?"

"I just turned it on. They haven't said."

Jax sat down on the bed and leaned against the headboard. He was inches away from her. She shared this bed with her husband. The old familiar guilt crept in, but she pushed it away. Life had changed for her, and there was nothing that she could do about it. Nate was gone, and right now she needed Jax…was thankful for him. She had to quit allowing the flashbacks.

"Well, it looks like this isn't going to go away quietly."

Her mind wandered, and she missed the forecast. "What did they say?"

Jax glanced over at her, taking his eyes from the television. "Are you sure you want me in here? I could sleep out in the hall, and I'd still be close."

She swallowed hard, grabbing her pillow in front of her. "I need you here." She said it so softly, she wondered if he heard her.

"Then this is where I'll be," he answered in a low voice. "Where's the junk food you were talking about?"

"Back in what they used to call a kitchen."

"Let's go pick some stuff out and watch a movie. What do you say?"

Brynn loved his enthusiasm for everything he did. Whether it was working in the castle, looking for missing computers, or trying to take her mind off her troubles, he always gave it his all. "I have popcorn and a microwave."

He grinned. "Let's do this."

He moved from the bed and held his hand out to her. She hesitated momentarily, but then she reached out to him. Once she was on her feet, he didn't let go but pulled her to him. Their mouths were inches apart. They stood like that for what seemed an eternity. How she wished she could throw caution to the wind and demand the kiss she ached for. Instead she allowed him to lead her to the kitchen, never letting go of her hand.

Brynn missed the warmth, the closeness of a man she loved. She was completely aware of the sensation of her hand in his. She wanted more from this man, who had become something more than a friend. The question was what was he to her? Was she grateful? Was it hero worship? Or was she falling in love? How could she be falling in love with another man, when she never stopped loving Nate?

They reached the kitchen, and she leaned against the counter, pulling her hand from his. She made no move to get the snacks they were there for. Her mind was swirling with questions.

"Hey, sunshine, what's on your mind?"

She bit down on her lip. Did she spill her feelings? Was she ready for rejection? "I'm good." Brynn turned away and rummaged through a cupboard.

His hands were warm on her hips, pivoting her toward him. "Brynn?"

He had a way of making her legs go to jelly. "I'm…uh…I don't know what to say."

"How about what you're thinking?"

She stepped away. She needed distance to gather her thoughts. "I'm trying to confront some things."

"And?"

"God, this is hard." She rested her hand on her forehead, trying to find the words. "I love Nate."

"He was your husband. I get that."

Why now was she noticing the biceps under the white t-shirt he was wearing? "Maybe I'm not ready for this conversation."

Jax placed his hands on her shoulders, and dropped his head to look into her eyes. "Talk to me. I promise it will do us both good."

She lowered herself onto a nearby stool, not knowing how long her legs would hold her up. "I'm not sure how I feel, so I'm just going to talk. I warn you, I'll probably make no sense." Shifting on the stool, she allowed the words to flow. “I loved Nate. I still love him, but lately I notice you more and more. I’m not sure if I’m grateful, or if what I’m feeling is the beginning of something more.”

His expression was impossible to read. “Maybe I can help. When I’m not with you, do you wish I was here? Do you find yourself counting the minutes until we’re together? Do you wonder what your life would be with me?” He didn’t wait for her answer, but continued, “Because, if you do any of those things than we’re on exactly the same page.”

“I do all those things. But I’m also consumed with guilt. How could I be forgetting a husband I considered the love of my life?” She swiped at a stray tear.

“I doubt very much you’re forgetting him. I wouldn’t ask you to, but I’d ask you to give me a chance to bring love back into your life.”

Jax made no attempt to close the space between them. “How can I expect you to share my heart with my deceased husband? You deserve more than that.”

“Brynn, I’m not going to pretend I know what you’re going through, because I don’t. I do know that I have some pretty strong feelings for you. And I think, if we’re meant to be, our love will become the center of your life. You’ll never forget what you had with Nate. He’s part of who you are, and I’m good with that.” He paused for a moment before adding, “Are you falling in love with me?”

“I’m not sure. How do I know? You’re my knight in shining armor here. You’re protecting me, helping me…what if I’m feeling hero worship?”

He chuckled with a raised eyebrow. “Nate was a cop, and so was I. Maybe you have a thing for cops?”

She blew out a frustrated sigh.

"Do we really have to define it? What if we enjoyed each other's company and let things unravel the way they're supposed to?"

"I don't want to get hurt again. I don't think I could bare another loss." There. She said it.

"I can understand that. I'm sure you've heard there's no guarantees in life, right?" He stood in front of her now, resting his hands on the counter, one on each side of her. She had nowhere to run.

"I did hear that somewhere, yes." Her voice was barely above a whisper. Her eyes found his. Big mistake. The blood pounded in her ears as he lowered his lips to hers. So, so soft…so gentle with her. She held her breath. The kiss was brief, but the most sensual she'd ever encountered. "Jax, I…"

He placed an index finger against her lips. "No. You can analyze this later. For now, let's enjoy the moment."

Chapter Thirty-Three

They ate popcorn and drank wine while watching a stupid comedy on TV. They laughed, talked about nothing related to ghosts, bad guys, or break-ins, and enjoyed each other's company. For the first time in a long time, she relaxed. Brynn had fallen asleep half way through. She totally missed the uncomfortable part of him sliding under the covers with her. When she awoke, he was already gone from the room. A moment of panic passed through her, but it was brief. He wouldn't leave her. She grabbed her furry robe and left her room to search for him.

Jax was painting in her new quarters. She quietly observed him, enjoying a few moments of uninterrupted voyeurism. He was an insanely handsome man. She noticed that from the start, but now Brynn was thinking of him in different terms. Maybe he could be her insanely handsome man? No more thinking, and to make sure of that, she cleared her throat to gain his attention.

He turned and grinned. "Finally up, sleepy head?"

"I don't usually sleep in like this."

Jax closed the distance between them and wrapped his arms around her, kissing the top of her head. "I missed you."

Her stomach rolled. Was it with dread, or excitement?

Leaving an arm around her shoulder, and facing the room, he asked, "What do you think of the color you picked?"

The light sage on the walls personalized her little corner of the castle. It was her favorite color. She intended on her living space to be slightly more modern than elsewhere in the castle. The crown molding had already been painted by a previous owner, so she was satisfied with the fresh paint that accented the walls. Jax had done an amazing job with the wood mantel fireplace. It now held a dark stain. This had been servants' quarters, so nothing was as elaborate as the front of the castle. The leaded windows with stained glass across the tops were only found in old homes, like this castle. Her windows shared the same opulence as the rest of the mansion. It was important for continuity outside looking in. She looked forward to the day when the sun actually made an appearance—she was going to be blown away by the rays dancing through the glass.

"This is everything I hoped it would be." She hugged him.

"I should have the room painted by the end of the day. When the town is up and running again, we can schedule the carpet for the bedroom. Do you still want carpet in here too?"

"I've thought about it quite a bit, and yeah, I do. I'm going for homey. I can always change my mind."

"You should be able to move in here soon."

"I'll have to give Brad a call, and ask if there are any updates on my order." Jax's face tightened at the mention of Brad's name. "Are you jealous?" She couldn't hide the smirk.

"I don't trust him."

"You think he'll make a pass at me?"

"Oh, I don't think, I know. It's just a matter of when. And then, I'll have to try to control my animal instincts." He picked up the paint can and emptied some in the tray.

"What if I told you, if he makes a pass at me, I'll let you handle it?"

"I must disclose that handling it might include a fist to his face."

She attempted to hide the smile that threatened an appearance. "Whatever you decide."

"Really? So, does that mean something has changed between us?"

"Would you like it to?" Her face burned with embarrassment. It had been a long time, since she'd danced this dance.

"Yeah. The next time we go out in public, I want everyone to know that Brynn Austin is mine."

"I might be okay with that. You can start with Brad." She exited without further comment.

Sebastian was waiting in the rotunda when she headed back to her room. In the bright sunshine she imagined him hard to see, but with today's dark cloud cover she had no problem. "Good morning, Sebastian."

Her friendly ghost followed her into her room. "I couldn't help, but overhear your conversation with Mr. Maddox. You're an item now?"

"You were eavesdropping again? Sebastian, I'm surprised at you. A man with your credentials hovering outside the door, listening to other people's conversations, I would never have expected that."

He pulled at his suit coat and stood straight as a board. "I was searching for you. I heard your voice and didn't want to interrupt. I must say, I'm pleased."

She lowered herself onto her bed. "I hope I'm doing the right thing. I don't want to lead Jax on. What if I find these feelings are not really of the romantic kind, but of gratefulness?"

"I see the way you look at each other. I'm not worried about that outcome. I have told Mr. Maddox he has my blessing. You are of marriageable age. What else could I say? My dear, I was not blessed with a daughter, but if I had been I would have been so proud of a girl like yourself." With a wave of the hand, he changed the subject. "At any rate, that's not why I dropped by. I was wondering if you've had a chance to read through Helena's journal?"

Touched by the admission, Brynn couldn't let his comment slip by without notice. "I care about you, too, Sebastian. I forget that you're not of this world. I think there's something better waiting for you, but if there's not I would be honored to share this castle with you until they carry me out of here." He nodded sharply, and appeared uncomfortable with all the sentiment. "Now, about Helena's journal…I've not read much of it yet, with all that's been going on. Have you changed your mind? Would you like it returned to the attic?"

"No, dear, that's not my wish. I'd like you to read it. I've had it in my hands many times, but couldn't bring myself to look at the pages. What if there's something that would doom the beautiful memories I have? I want to know what happened to her, but I can't read her words."

"I will. But, Sebastian, is there anything you don't want to know?" She didn't want to be the one to break her friend's heart.

"If she ran off with that vile man, I need to know. The details are not necessary."

"I understand. I think I'll curl up over here and start reading. The storm's supposed to last a couple of days. It's the perfect time to devote to this."

"Thank you, Brynn." With that he faded into the air. She only prayed any news she gave him would be good.

Chapter Thirty-Four

I deeply regret my decision to show favor to Mr. Hammond. I have shamed the man I swore my allegiance. Since retrieving me from the party, he has not made an appearance. All has happened, because of my desperation. My husband seems to have forgotten my existence. His heart, where once it was filled with love for me, has now been filled with the need for revenge against Mr. Hammond. He will not stop until he sees his demise. I had hoped if Mr. Hammond showered his attentions on me, my husband would once again notice me. He was once such a kind soul. I'm not quite sure when the dark side took root, but it is very clear that he is only content with his ships, his inventions, and the need to be king of his castle. I would gladly give every penny to have my dearest Sebastian back with me.

H.M.

Brynn's eyes filled with tears. Helena had loved Sebastian very much, but her loneliness led to a desperate act of betrayal. She couldn't help wonder how far her relationship with Jonathan Hammond had gone. Three knocks echoed through the room, pulling her eyes from the journal. She found Jax leaning against the doorjamb.

"You hungry? I was going to heat up some of that soup." He walked over to the chair and looked down at her. "Why have you been crying?"

"I'm not." Not technically.

"Your nose is red, and your eyes look…"

"How? How do they look?"

"Like you've been crying. Did I do something to upset you? Because I'm a guy and we have a knack for that."

"You're safe. I'm reading Helena's journal. She loved Sebastian, but she was desperate to get him to notice her."

"I always noticed her." Sebastian spoke from behind Jax. "It would seem she was not aware of that."

How did she tell her friend that he drove his wife to another man? The waterworks were threatening a repeat performance. "I don't know much. Why don't you let me finish, and then we'll talk."

"You're reading about the night of the dinner party. I refused to go but had a change of heart. I arrived at the party to find Helena in the arms of my enemy, Jonathan Hammond." The way Sebastian uttered his name showed his contempt for the man. "I insisted she leave with me immediately. We stayed in seclusion for a week. It was when I returned to the shipyard she disappeared."

"Did you speak that week?" Jax asked.

"Very little. I could barely stand to look at her. She stayed in her rooms." The drooping of Sebastian's shoulders spoke volumes. "If only I'd spoken to her, discussed what happened. She disappeared and so did Jonathan Hammond. I was led to believe one thing—they ran off together. I was questioned extensively by detectives but never charged. They searched this castle for anything to incriminate me but found nothing. It wasn't for the lack of trying. I did not kill my wife. I never knew if she lived or died."

"I'm going to keep reading. Maybe something will turn up."

"Soup, Brynn?"

"No, thanks. I'll grab something later."

****

Brynn Austin was a kind woman. With all the problems at her feet, she took the time to help out a ghost from another century. Her life could be in danger, but instead she was worrying about Sebastian.

Jax took a bite of the soup and opened the computer. He tried a few more potential passwords, and all were denied. If only he could get to his place and pick up the flash drive. He could unlock this thing in no time. His gut told him once these roads were passable, they'd be getting another visit.

"No luck, Mr. Maddox?"

"No, Sebastian, I'm afraid not. It's doable. I just don't have what I need here. I'm afraid they'll be back soon." Jax walked over to the window and watched the snow fall. It was a bit lighter, but the weather station called for more wind and whiteout conditions through tomorrow.

"I believe the computer should be returned to the passageways for safe keeping. And maybe we should come up with a plan of action."

"What are you thinking?"

"If these hoodlums manage to break into the castle, we should have an escape route mapped. There are two more entrance points. I've shown you the one off the ladies' reception room, and the one from the solarium outside Brynn's current bedroom, or what *used* to be my dining room. And you have seen the wine cellar entry. Follow me." Jax followed him to the grand staircase right off the rotunda. It appeared to be an exquisitely carved wall, but with one push of a single wooden panel, a door flipped open. "I know you can't see the descent, but there are conventional stairs leading to the passageway. Come this way." Jax did without question.

They traveled back through the rotunda and into the large living room, which was so mammoth, Jax had trouble imagining it as a place to kick back and relax. A large bookcase stood at the far end of the room. Naturally, with a simple pull, it opened like a door. "This is a secret room. It would be suitable for a temporary hiding place, but it doesn't lead anywhere. Perhaps, you could hide the computer in this room?"

Would someone figure this room was here? He'd been in here more times than he could count and never had a suspicion. He considered himself an observant guy. "I think it would work. So, what's your suggested plan of action?"

"If they gain entrance, you take Brynn to the closest entrance point to the passageways. I'll hold them off with my charms." It was one of the rare times Jax saw Sebastian smile. "I'll get them out of here. You just have to keep her hidden. Do you still have your weaponry?"

"On me at all times. Be ready, Sebastian. It's going to happen."

"I know, son, I know."

Chapter Thirty-Five

The voices of Jax and Sebastian drifted into her room more than once, but she paid no mind. She read on.

Sebastian has scarcely said a word to me, since our return from the party. I deserve his silence, but I can no longer live in this manner. Jonathan has promised me a life abroad. I could start fresh. No one would know me. I have told him I would never be able to marry, at least not right away. I do not love Mr. Hammond, but he promises me I will be cherished. What more can a woman want? Sebastian no longer loves me. My heart aches, and my tears fall upon this paper. We shall leave in two days' time. I will take nothing with me. Jonathan will have a trunk filled with my necessities, and I will purchase new when we arrive. I hope Sebastian finds the happiness he deserves.

H.M.

Brynn couldn't believe it. She *had* left. How was she going to break this to Sebastian?

I've changed my mind…I don't want to go through with this. I explained to Jonathan my love for Sebastian runs too deeply. I could never love him. It's not fair for him to live with a woman who loves another.

Brynn thought of Jax. Was she doing the same thing? Trying to replace her love with another? Trying to hide her heartache?

At first, he attempted to convince me with kindness, but threats soon followed. He will kill my precious Sebastian if I do not travel with him to France. How can I put my love in jeopardy? I must do what he asks. I only have myself to blame for my unhappiness, and that of my husband's. My only hope is he will find love with another someday. My fate will lie with Jonathan Hammond. Someday I will be his wife, and bear his children. This is what he wants of me, and I shall do my penance. I pray one day Sebastian Morgan will forgive me.

H.M.

Her hands shook as she closed the last page of the journal. Helena had been coerced, threatened to comply with Jonathan Hammond's demands. If she could find the name of the ship and maybe a manifest, she might be able to find out where they landed and follow a trail. So much of this was available on line. She had sidetracked herself one day on an ancestry site and found pictures of the ships her relatives had arrived on. According to Helena they were going to France. She couldn't help but wonder if Helena hadn't recorded all of this in the journal in hopes Sebastian would read it and come to find her.

Brynn's stomach growled, and she decided a bowl of soup was better than nothing. She nearly smacked right into Jax, bundled up in winter garb. "Where are you going?"

"I'm going to dig us out of here. If I wait much longer, my plow won't handle it."

"By digging us out, aren't you allowing them in?"

"I suppose that's one way of looking at it, but I have to get the flash drive I need to get through that password. Eventually, they're going to be able to get here anyway. I want to be ready for them on every level."

Brynn second-guessed her reluctance of including the police. "Maybe we should call the local police. We could always ask them not to notify the NYPD."

"They're bound too, Brynn. I can handle this. I'm trained. We'll call the FBI as soon as we see what's on that computer. Trust me?"

She nodded. "I do. But I don't want anything to happen to you, because I draggedyou into something you had nothing to do with. I would never forgive myself."

Jax moved within inches of her, shadowing her with his height. "Let's get one thing clear. You did not drag me into this. I walked in willingly. I've been clear about my feelings for you, and I've been clear I expect nothing in return. But I will not leave you alone in this. We're going to finish this together. Once this is over, maybe you'll be able to move forward...with, or without me. But you have to know, your dream has become mine, Brynn."

Brynn trembled. She couldn't be sure if it was his close proximity, or the words that went straight to her heart. In many ways Jax Maddox was very much like Nate. They were both strong, honorable men who did right by others. Without thought, she wrapped her arms around him. She sighed when his arms encircled her in return.

"Ahem."

Brynn jumped back. Did ghosts really have to clear their throats?

"I apologize for the interruption, but the voice on

the radio suggested the storm may be coming to an end by morning."

"I was afraid of that." The serious look on Jax's face didn't do much for her nerves. He spoke directly to Brynn. "I'm going to plow us out of here. We'll go to my house and get what we need as soon as I'm finished. I don't care if I have to push through the snow all the way there."

She found it hard to swallow, let alone speak.

"Brynn, don't worry. I'm not going to let anything happen to you."

She watched him walk out the door. She wasn't worried about herself. In that instance, she knew if anything happened to him she would die alongside of him.

****

Brynn glanced out the cloak room window. He'd been out there awhile. She sighed and leaned her head against the windowpane.

"He's in love with you, you know."

"Sebastian, you need to quit sneaking up on me. Rattle some chains, or something."

"Don't change the subject, my girl."

"I wasn't."

"You were. Might I give you a bit of advice?" He didn't wait for a reply. "I made some grave mistakes with my Helena, and it would seem I'm paying my penance now."

Brynn's thoughts went to Helena's journal entry, where she made reference to the very same thing. How was she ever going to tell Sebastian what she learned?

"That man loves you. I know you still grieve for your departed. You're a good and loyal woman, but you're here and he's not. I would wager he would tell you the same. I have to believe he was a good man to deserve such devotion from you. Brynn, you have your life ahead of you. There are adventures to be had, children to raise, a life to live. Mr. Maddox would give you all those things, if you'd allow him."

Sebastian stood next to her at the window. Brynn didn't have to see him to know he was there. The cold that surrounded him always indicated his presence. Jax was finally returning, and her heart skipped with anticipation. The corners of her mouth turned up slightly at the sight of him. Sebastian was right. She couldn't pinpoint when, but he had opened her heart again. When this was all over, she'd tell him. For now, they had to focus.

Chapter Thirty-Six

Jax walked in and shook the snow off of him. It was falling at a good clip. Brynn brushed his coat off with her hands, and shivered. "Do you think it's a good idea to leave now? What if you get stuck?"

"It took me some time to push through all of it, but yeah, I think this is the perfect time. They're less likely to be out in this. I have to have that flash drive. I don't want an unexpected rendezvous with them. If they're going to make their move, I want it to be on our terms. And it's not going to be *me.* It's going to be *us.* Go bundle up. We're going on a road trip."

Brynn exited without argument. She didn't want separated from Jax, not ever. It was time to face that fact.

Sebastian had remained silent, until that moment. "Do you think it's wise to take her with you?"

"I vowed I wasn't going to let her out of my sight until this is wrapped up. I'm sticking to that. I can't protect her if she's not with me."

"You don't trust me to care for her in your absence?"

"It's nothing against your ability. I'm confident you would scare the hell out of someone who walked in here. I can't explain why I need her with me."

"You love her."

"She's not ready for that."

"Maybe not now, but don't give up on her. She's getting there."

"You think?"

Before Sebastian could comment, Brynn returned. She could make a winter coat look sexy. "You ready?"

"Yep. Let's do this. Sebastian? You'll hold down the fort?"

"I will, my dear. You two have a care."

Jax opened the door and waited for her to climb in. He fired up the truck and glanced over. He had never fallen for anyone this hard. Yeah, she was *the one*, and he'd wait as long as it took for her to realize it too. For now, his focus needed to be on the task at hand. Even though he didn't expect to be followed, or worse, he was ready. The weight of his firearm, firmly at his side, reminded him of the seriousness of what could happen.

The usual fifteen minute trip to his house took forty five, but they arrived safely and without incident.

"Jax…this is gorgeous." He glanced over to see Brynn gaping openly out the windshield. "You built this, didn't you?"

"A few years back. My dream was to live away from the chaos of life."

"That was ours too." He knew she referred to Nate. "We wanted to get away from city life. Danger was such a part of our lives. It would seem I can't get away from it. Not even here."

Jax turned in the seat to face her. He took her hand in his before saying, "I promise you, Brynn, we're going to finish this, so you get that life you wanted." His lips lightly grazed the back of her hand. "Let's go in."

Jax's eyes roamed the entire area in front of them,

searching for anything out of the ordinary. Satisfied, he exited the truck, and Brynn followed. He released his firearm from his holster. “Stay close, and stay behind me.” Placing his key in the lock, he slowly opened the front door and peered in. Nothing looked amiss. Jax closed the door behind them and turned the deadbolt. “Do *not* leave my side.” He wasn’t totally convinced they were alone—just the nature of his training.

Jax moved through the house quickly, searching every room. Satisfied, he retrieved the item he needed. “Okay. Let’s get out of here.” His instincts were usually on the money, and right now the vibe wasn’t good.

He moved them quickly to the truck and out the driveway.

“Jax, is something wrong? Did you see something?”

“No, didn’t see anything…just a feeling.”

Brynn made no reply and remained silent beside him. The return trip was a bit faster, and again, he was on high alert driving down the lane to the castle. They made it back in and were greeted by Sebastian.

“Did you retrieve what you needed?” The anxious tone was mirrored by the fading in and out of his image. They all knew their reprieve was ending with the snowstorm, and they had little time to prepare.

Jax held up the flash drive.

“You would be best to move quickly, Mr. Maddox. I’m not getting a good feeling.”

“Yeah. Me either.” He looked to Brynn. “I’m going into the secret room in the living room. If you hear even a snowflake fall, you come and get me. Understand?”

She glanced out the window, then back at him. “The snow’s still falling. I think we’re good for a while yet. I'm going to see if I can get creative for dinner."

"I'm serious, Brynn. Anything. You come and get me."

"I will. I promise."

Satisfied, Jax headed for the secret room, and Sebastian followed. This could be the beginning of the end of this mess. He just hoped Nate Austin had what they needed on this computer.

****

The stove in the kitchen was old, but functional. Brynn hadn't stocked the refrigerator, but she had a few things she could possibly create something from. Anything, but soup. She lost herself in the preparation. Focusing on something besides impending doom quieted her nerves. Could it be? She almost felt optimistic…

Brynn had enjoyed cooking for Nate. She thought back to the dinners they shared. She knew how to set a table, complete with candles. Nate's days were stressful, and Brynn did what she could to create a calm, peaceful place for him. She threw open a couple of drawers and searched for candles. At this point, she didn't care if he got the wrong idea, because maybe it wasn't the wrong idea at all.

She opened the third drawer in her search, and heard something behind her. A hand came over her mouth before she had the chance to turn. Cold steel rested against her temple. She knew before he spoke. Apollo Banks had found her.

Chapter Thirty-Seven

A strange calm flowed through her. She knew it was coming, and it was almost a relief. She would not be intimidated by this man. She would not show him fear. He ruined her life, and she was angry. No…that wasn't the word for it.

"If you scream, I'll shoot you right here," he hissed. He removed his hand from her mouth, and grabbed her arm, turning her to face him. The gun was in her face. "Where's your boyfriend?"

"He's not my boyfriend. He's working somewhere in the castle. I wasn't keeping tabs on him."

"Listen, bitch. I'm in no mood to play games. He walks in here, and I'll shoot him, just like I did your last one."

Brynn grabbed the counter behind her. The comment went straight to her heart. She had to think of something. "What do you want?"

"My computer's missing, and I want it back. That's it. I get it back, you and your boyfriend live. Simple enough, right?"

Brynn nearly slipped and said she didn't have his computer, she had Nate's. She inhaled slowly, attempting to calm her nerves. She needed to think, but it was hard to do with a gun to your forehead. "Would you get that out of my face? What am I going to do? Outrun you?"

"I'll give you one thing…you're a gutsy ho."

Her hand itched to connect to his face. A face she was committing to memory. His long dreadlocks with beads pulled back in a ponytail. And the eyes…she'd never forget looking into his eyes, full of plain evil.

His hand tightly encircled her upper arm, and with a vise grip, he dragged her into the rotunda. She hoped it was Sebastian that would hear them first, and scare the life right out of him. If Jax came up to investigate, Apollo would kill him. He was a cold-blooded murderer.

"Are you going to tell me where my computer is, or am I gonna have to beat it out of you? Because I'd enjoy bouncin' you around."

"That would be a very bad idea."

Brynn's eyes darted in the direction of his voice, coming from the ladies' drawing room. Somehow, he'd made it across the hall without being seen. Her heart thumped with dread. Apollo had nothing to lose.

"I'll blow her brains out, just like I did her husband," he threatened.

"Again, that would be a very bad idea. You'd have nothing to negotiate with, and I'd have nothing to lose. I'll kill you."

The tone in Jax's voice was foreign to Brynn. All the kindness was gone. She trusted Jax with her life, but how were they going to get out of this?

And when she thought there was no hope, Sebastian floated down the hallway in their direction. Apollo's mouth dropped, and fear crossed his face. Romeo landed on Apollo's back with a loud yowl, followed by a series of screams from her captor. Brynn assumed her cat had dug his claws in, but she didn't stick around long enough to find out. Apollo dropped his gun, and she took full advantage of it, running to Jax and the cover of the drawing room. Romeo took off up the steps.

Jax pushed her behind him. They weren't out of the woods, but at least she was at Jax's side, and no longer a bargaining chip. "It's over, Banks. The castle ghost isn't going to let you out of here."

Sebastian spoke. "How dare you come in my home and hold a gun to my friend."

Apollo backed up against the wall, his eyes as large as saucers. He pointed the gun at Sebastian and fired. Sebastian laughed. "You want to try again, young man? I think you missed." Apollo fired again, and Sebastian floated around the rotunda taunting him.

Obviously aware he wasn't able to kill something already dead, he turned his gun in their direction and pulled the hammer back. The sound of it echoed throughout the rotunda. With no time to process what was happening around her, the single gunshot fired. Brynn squeezed her eyes shut and slid down the wall in a kneeling position. This couldn't be happening again. She slipped away from reality.

****

"Brynn? Baby, it's okay. Open your eyes. It's over." Jax's voice broke the barrier, and she cautiously opened her eyes.

Was it possible? Jax was really okay? He kneeled in front of her, waiting for her to fall apart, but she wasn't going to. She grabbed him instead and held him tightly. He spoke quietly in her ear. She wasn't sure what. She didn't care. He was alive, and so was she.

Sebastian spoke, interrupting her jubilation.

"Excuse me, but the hoodlum is bleeding all over my rotunda."

For the first time since the sound of the gunshot, the groans of her husband's killer filled her ears, and she felt nothing—no compassion, no remorse, but to her surprise, no satisfaction. The only thing she felt was love…love for the man who had just saved her life. And love for a ghost, that lived almost a century before her.

In no time, the castle overflowed with local police and paramedics. Brynn had thought she even saw a firefighter walk by. She sat quietly on the window seat in the living room, watching the pandemonium in front of her. Apollo Banks had been taken to the hospital. He would survive. Jax hadn't shot to kill but to stop him. *Jax.* She sighed. She hadn't really gotten to talk to him, before her home was invaded. Her home…and Sebastian's, who was also laying low. If it wouldn't have been for her friendly ghost, they might not be alive. Brynn would be forever grateful. She stared out the window. How was she going to tell him Helena had left with Jonathan Hammond, not because she wanted to, but because she felt she had no other choice? This news wasn't going to bring the closure she was hoping for. Brynn had hoped he'd find the peace he was searching for and be able to move on. Well, if that didn't happen, she'd be content with him living here with her at the castle.

"Brynn?"

Her head snapped in Jax's direction, and she stood. He wasn't alone.

"This is FBI agent, Wayne Tolliver. He'd like to talk to you about your husband." Jax turned to leave.

“Jax, don’t go.” She grabbed his arm, looking up at him, pleading with her eyes. To her relief, he stayed at her side. She extended her hand to the agent.

“Mrs. Austin…”

“Brynn, please.” This was her transition. She would always be grateful for the time she had with Nate. He had taught her what a husband should be. And she would always love him, but he was now a memory…a memory she would cherish and hold with her forever. But Sebastian was right. She lived, and she still had dreams. She prayed wherever Nate was he would understand.

Chapter Thirty-Eight

They sat in the unfinished living room—she, Jax, and the FBI agent. Jax showed Agent Tolliver the evidence Nate had compiled on Banks. It was quite extensive and thorough. The computer, as it turned out, wasn't Nate's. Somewhere along the line, Nate had switched the computers. They were identical, and it had fooled Banks for a while. Her husband was quite the genius. It should have worked. Nate should be here, finishing his case. He should be telling the agent Apollo Banks was the ringleader of a weapons ring—that copycat weapons were made and funneled to him from outside the country.

Brynn listened as Agent Tolliver explained the local police were involved with his investigation, but the NYPD was going to be kept out pending an inquiry of their involvement, if any. He assured her the police commissioner would cooperate fully with federal officers. They were fairly sure someone had sold Nate out. They may never know who that someone was, and Brynn had to make peace with that.

Agent Tolliver stood to leave. "Mrs. Austin, your husband was a hero in my book. Those guns get in the hands of kids. They're used in crimes, murders, drug deals… He closed one lane of traffic. We'll honor him, by continuing his fight. And thank you, both of you, for your part."

"It was all Jax. I couldn't have survived this without him." She smiled up at him with a heart full of gratitude.

"You should have called us right away, but I guess that's water under the bridge. And, Mr. Maddox, if you ever consider joining the bureau, I'll put in a good word for you."

Jax chuckled. "Thanks, but no. I have a castle to finish."

The first relaxed feeling of happiness passed over Brynn in a long time. "He's not going anywhere. I can't finish this without him."

Jax's arm rested over her shoulder while they watched the agent leave. Slowly, one by one, they left until Jax and Brynn were there alone. She walked over and looked at the blood-stained wood in her rotunda. She sighed.

"Blood on my rotunda floor. Never thought I'd see the day. Well, there was that one time with Jonathan Hammond…" Sebastian babbled on at her side, and her lips curled upward.

"I'll take care of it, Sebastian," Jax promised. "I'll sand it out right now."

"Wait," Brynn said urgently. "I want to thank both of you. Until I came here, I was alone in this. Without you two, I could've had a very different fate."

Sebastian spoke first. "I'm honored to have been of service to you, my lady. Assisting you was like helping my Helena. I failed her. I know that. You needn't worry about telling me. I've seen it in your eyes. You didn't want to tell me what you read."

"You know?"

"Yes, my dear. I watched you reading her words. I

saw the tears in your eyes, and the sympathy when I spoke of her. I did some reading myself, while you slept. I have much to do penance for. I will not complain about my sentence here on earth. It is generous, at best."

"Oh, Sebastian. Will you forgive me? I wanted to tell you. I was going to. Finding the right words…they wouldn't come."

"I understand, and there is nothing to forgive. If Helena and I would have ever had children, there would have been no greater blessing than to have a daughter such as yourself." He looked to Jax, who stood silently listening. "And you would make a fine son-in-law."

"Sebastian…" Jax warned.

"I believe now I will venture to the attic and rummage through our things. There might be something useful for our redecorating." He disappeared as quickly as he appeared.

"I want you to know I didn't put him up to that." Jax smiled sheepishly.

"I know. Sebastian has made it clear what he thinks."

"Oh, yeah? And what does he think?"

"That you'd make a good match for me."

"I agree."

"I think we need to talk." Brynn went to the closest place they could sit, the window seats in the living room. He deserved nothing but honesty.

Jax followed. "I don't think I like the sound of this."

She ignored the comment. "I have so many emotions swirling around right now. I don't know which way is up. In a way, I feel like I've just buried my husband again. I doubt that makes sense. The nightmare is finally over. I can put it behind me. I can look forward. And Jax? That scares me too. My heart wants to move forward with you, but there's guilt…so much of it. I love Nate. I always will, and how is that fair to you? I pray at night, asking him to give me a sign that he's okay with this. And all I get is silence."

He stood. "I appreciate the honesty. I'll get my stuff and be on my way."

"Jax, wait."

"I need to know what's in your head, sunshine. I love you, and I'm not sure I can go back to being just your general contractor."

"I have feelings for you," she blurted. "I'm afraid to call it love."

They stood facing each other, the silence loud between them.

"Maybe you need some time away from me to think clearly. I'll give orders to the crew, and the renovations will continue on schedule."

The last thing she wanted was time away from him, but he was right. Her thoughts were all jumbled. She needed to sort through the emotions, and time to say goodbye to Nate—to her old life. She nodded. "Okay. I appreciate that. Can I call you?"

"You let me know if there are any problems. I'll get with the crew leader."

"No, Jax, not for the renovation. Just to talk…to you." She missed him already.

"I'm going to miss you more than I can stand, but I think it would be best if you work through all this, Brynn, then call me."

Tears streamed down her face. This is not how she

thought the conversation would go. She moved toward him and held him close, closing her eyes and putting to memory the feel of his arms around her, the woodsy cologne that she would always associate with him, and the sound of his breathing.

He pulled away first and held her face in his hands, and lightly, for the first time, placed a gentle kiss on her lips. "I love you, sunshine. I hope, with time, you'll feel the same."

Jax left the room, never looking back, and walked down the hall, and out of her life.

Chapter Thirty-Nine

Weeks rolled into a month without seeing Jax. Brynn hoped her trips into town might produce an unexpected sighting, but it never did. Sebastian told her every day what a mistake she was making. But how could she have a real relationship with him when her heart still ached for her dead husband? She loved Jax, that was clear, but he deserved her whole heart, and she couldn't give him that—not yet, anyway.

So, she spent her days working on drawings, ordering wallpapers, and dealing with Brad, the Casanova. He'd got word that she wasn't seeing Jax, and he was falling all over her. He'd asked her to dinner, strictly business he'd said…and she'd agreed. Her hope was he'd see he wasn't going to get anywhere with her, and leave her alone. Now, she doubted the strategy as she dressed.

Brynn looked into the full-length mirror in the bedroom Jax had created for her. Her heart sank to an all new level. She had to end this misery. If she lost him forever, she had to know, but if there was a chance…it was time to tell him how she felt. She loved him, and any residual feeling of guilt would have to be dealt internally. She wasn't going to lose Jax. Her decision was made.

She pulled down on the curve-hugging little black dress she chose, knowing this was a bad choice, but not having anything else appropriate for the high-end restaurant Brad had chosen. The doorbell sounded from below. She hurried down the steps, knowing, if given a chance, Sebastian would answer the door and give him the fright of his life. And somehow, she didn't think that was good for business.

Brynn opened the door, and Brad gave out a low whistle. "You look amazing. I'm going to have the hottest date there."

"It's not a date, Brad. It's a business meeting." She regretted this already.

"Call it what you want, but I'm going to enjoy myself either way."

She stifled a groan. "Let me get my coat. I'll be right back." She went around the corner to the cloak room and pulled down her dress coat. She slipped into it, turned to leave, and was greeted with the disapproving look of her resident ghost.

"Have you lost all your good sense?"

"Shhh! It's business, that's it," she whispered.

"I've seen that look, and he doesn't have business on his mind."

"I can handle him."

He responded with an angry look and evaporated into thin air. She was used to it now.

"Who were you talking to?" Brad asked.

"Oh, myself. I couldn't reach the coat I wanted. The hooks in this place are up so high."

He shot her a suspicious look but let the conversation end there. "Shall we go?"

Brynn turned to pull the door closed, and there stood Sebastian with his arms snugly across his chest.

Brynn made the appropriate comments to Brad's

constant conversation. He was obviously impressed with his Cadillac. Her head was already pounding, and they hadn't walked into the restaurant yet.

Brad parked, jumped out of the car, and quickly came around to open her door. He was pulling out all the stops. "Do you do this for your male business acquaintances?"

"If they were as gorgeous as you, yeah, I would."

Brynn rolled her eyes. His hand rested under her elbow as they ascended the stairs. They were greeted, and the door was opened for them. Brynn and Nate were not high society, and she wasn't in her comfort zone.

Brad was asked his name for the reservation, and they were swiftly taken to the dining room. Her eyes met his as she approached his table. She wanted the ground to swallow her up, and put her out of her misery, but instead Jax stood and she had no other choice, but to stop. "Jax." She forced a smile.

Jax glanced at Brad, then back to her. He made no attempt to hide his disapproval. "You look…nice," he said with a raised eyebrow, and a scowl.

Brynn responded with a quiet "thank you", before biting down on her lip.

"Darling, are you going to introduce us to your friends?"

For the first time, Brynn noticed the couple sitting with Jax at his table, an older couple with kind faces.

"I'm sorry, Mom. I didn't mean to be rude. This is Brynn Austin. She owns the castle my crew has been renovating."

No mention that he once told her he loved her.

Brad reached over to shake the hand of Jax's

father. "I'm Brad. The dinner date. Ma'am." He acknowledged Jax's mom with a nod and a smile.

Brynn couldn't let this go on. "Actually, Brad and I are here for a business meeting. He's doing the furnishings for the castle."

"Oh, that's wonderful," his mother exclaimed. "I'd love to see what you've done. I love historic places. Maybe Jax can run us over before we leave town."

Brynn smiled. "I'd like that."

"Mom, I'm sure Brynn..." he corrected himself, "Mrs. Austin, is very busy."

"I'd love the visit, and your impression on what we've done." She flashed a challenging look in Jax's direction. "I'm renovating it into a bed and breakfast."

"Jax, dear, could you fit that into your schedule tomorrow before we leave?"

He faced Brynn, with his back to his mother, and glared. "Sure. I'll check in on the crew while you take a tour." The icy stare he gave her was proof enough he didn't buy her explanation on why she was here with Brad.

"I'll look forward to it." She returned the stare, before gazing over his shoulder. "Enjoy your dinner, Mr. and Mrs. Maddox."

Brad wrapped his arm around her waist, leading her away from the table. She said in a low voice, "If you don't remove your hand from my waist, I'm going to make a scene." His arm immediately dropped to his side. For there was one thing she knew, Casanova liked to impress.

To his credit, he behaved the rest of dinner. That was after she threatened to take her business elsewhere. And if there was one thing Brad enjoyed more than impressing people, it was money. Because without it, he couldn't put on a show.

Jax left shortly after they were seated, and her mind wandered no matter how hard she tried to focus. Naturally, he was thinking the worst of her. She could see it in his eyes. Would he believe her? His mother was visiting, and she knew she wouldn't get one moment alone with him. He was angry, and he'd avoid her.

Brad drove her home and walked her to the door. "Are you going to ask me in?"

"No, I'm not. You tried to make this something it wasn't, and I'm considering taking my business elsewhere. This has been an uncomfortable evening."

"I apologize, Brynn. The way you're dressed. I thought you had more in mind."

"I dressed for a dinner at a high-end restaurant. Jax was right about you. I didn't listen." She shook her head. "You know what? Just cancel my future orders." She opened the door.

"Hey, if you want to hang with the low end, that's fine by me."

Brynn responded with a bright smile. "Tonight, I did that. I don't care for it. Goodnight."

Chapter Forty

Brynn closed the door behind her and leaned against it. She fought tears with everything she had.

"You're home early," Sebastian commented, floating toward her. "Are you crying? What did that man do to you?" His voice raised an octave.

"Nothing I couldn't handle. Jax was there." Her eyes pooled with the threat of an overflow.

"Oh, no. This can't be good. What happened?" He led her into the living room, now beautifully decorated.

Brynn lowered herself on the couch she first saw in the attic, buried under dust. So much had changed since then, symbolized by the new upholstery that covered it. She grabbed a tissue from the side table and dabbed her eyes. "He assumed I was on a date with Brad."

"Well, I can see how he'd assume that." She shot Sebastian a look. "My dear, you're not exactly in business attire."

He was right, and the feeling of hopelessness increased. "He was with his parents. How am I going to fix this?"

"You will not handle this the way I did with Helena. Silence isn't the answer. You will contact him, and explain. You will accept his anger for what it is…hurt. He has done everything to accommodate your feelings. He has stepped aside to allow you time to grieve, and he finds you at a romantic restaurant with his competition? Oh, Brynn…history does repeat itself."

"I was not at a romantic restaurant, and I was not trying to hurt him for his attention. I didn't know he was going to be there. This is not you and Helena revisited. This is my life, and I'm going to have to take charge of it."

"On that, we agree. And you should do it immediately." And, *poof,* he was gone.

Brynn opened her purse and grabbed her cell. What was the right thing to do? The doorbell rang, interrupting her thoughts. She swore. If Brad thought he was going to talk her into giving him her business, he might as well turn around and go home. She flung the door open…and her mouth dropped.

"Jax," she said, barely above a whisper.

He didn't even ask to come in, walking right past her. "We need to talk."

"I was going to call you."

His eyebrows rose with surprise. "You were?"

"Yeah. Come into the living room." She reached up and grabbed one black, high-heeled pump from her aching feet, and then the other, before following him.

She turned on another light. "I want to apologize for this evening."

"Brynn, I don't want your apologies. I want to know what the hell you were doing with that guy. You know how I feel about you, and you know how I feel about that…"

She cut him off before the expletive. "I had no idea you were going to be there."

A hand went through his hair. "It's not whether you knew I'd be there, it's that you went with him at all. Did you not give me one damned thought?"

"I think about you every day. I thought you gave up on me."

"Jesus, Brynn. How many times, in how many different ways do I have to tell you I love you?" The frustration was obvious in his voice. It was somewhere between anger and exasperation.

"It wasn't a date."

"You were dressed for a date with someone you were trying to impress. I wanted to cover you up with my coat."

Brynn smiled inwardly. "I fired him."

"Good. So, now what?"

"I don't know, Jax."

"I sure as hell know. Neither one of you are leaving this room, until you hash out the details." Sebastian's voice boomed in a way Brynn had never heard before. He sounded…angry.

"This is a private conversation," Jax challenged.

The fireplace, at the end of the room, burst into flames. Brynn's eyes widened. Sebastian was losing his control.

"I've tried to be patient with the likes of both of you, but I'm at the end of the line. You love her…she loves you…stop the bellyaching and put an end to my misery."

Jax leaned forward, resting his arms on his knees, and looked in her direction. "You love me?"

She nodded.

He didn't move. His eyes pierced hers. "Say it."

Brynn exhaled the breath she held. "I love you."

He stood and pulled her to him. "It's settled then."

"What is?"

"I'm back on the crew, and the only dinners you'll be having are with me. Understood?"

"I can agree to that."

From the doorway, Sebastian spoke. "Let's make one thing clear. You are not moving back in here until you make an honest woman out of her. I won't give you a moment's peace, so don't try me."

"We'll do things your way, Sebastian. Now, I have to explain to my parents why the love of my life was having dinner with another man. You want to give us a moment alone?"

"Nothing inappropriate?"

"You said so yourself, Sebastian, I'm of marriageable age."

"That may be so, but you're not married. Mr. Maddox, I will trust your discretion."

Jax waited a moment before pulling her into the embrace she dreamed about every single day of his absence. "Do you know how long I've waited to kiss you? Really kiss you?"

"So, why are you talking?"

Brynn couldn't have anticipated anything more romantic, more sensual. She trembled from head to toe when he pulled his lips from hers. She reached up and gently touched his face. He brushed his lips softly across hers before saying, "Goodnight, Brynn."

She leaned against the wall and watched him walk out her front door. She knew she'd made the right decision when half of her heart left with him.

Chapter Forty-One

Months went by of renovations, decorating, fun, and laughter. The castle was coming together in the way she imagined. The old-world charm was successfully meeting comfort and the feeling of home she'd hoped for. Brynn couldn't have done it without Jax, or Sebastian. Jax's talent with renovation amazed her every day. His input was always right on the mark. And Sebastian's memories of life in the castle helped Brynn bring it back to life. He generously gave her his furniture and allowed her to refinish and reupholster as she saw fit.

"We should have a grand ball," Sebastian suggested out of the blue.

"With ball gowns and dancing?" Brynn's wheels turned. This could be a very good idea.

"Monkey suits?" Jax questioned.

"Monkey suits? No, my boy, tuxedoes. It shall be like the grand old days."

"I like the idea. Jax?"

"I'm not fond of a suit, but I'd do just about anything to see a smile on your face."

"Let's do it. You'll help plan it, Sebastian? I have no idea how to plan a ball. Oh, do you think anyone would come?"

Sebastian laughed. "They'll come. I'm sure people haven't changed all that much. If there's free food and entertainment, they'll trip over themselves getting here. Everyone wants to be seen at the event of the decade."

"Let's not settle with the event of the decade. Let's go for this century."

"I say, that's a splendid idea. The event of the century. You must put that on the invitations, Brynn. Let's start planning the menu."

Brynn laughed at his enthusiasm. It was nice seeing Sebastian happy for once. She wished she could do something to end his sorrow. But, for now, this was a good start.

****

Jax was working on one of the upstairs bedrooms, when he had a thought. Brynn was out and about making plans and ordering things for the party. It was the weekend, and the crew was gone for the day. "Sebastian?" he called.

He materialized right in front of him. "You rang?"

"I have an idea, and I'm going to need your help."

"At your service."

Jax smiled. "I was hoping you'd say that."

****

The invitations were sent, and Jax grumbled that most of the town was invited and would see him in a monkey suit. Her excitement grew with each passing day.

"Brynn, can I speak to you a minute?" Sebastian asked from the upper level of the rotunda. "Up here."

She glanced up, past the crystal chandelier that looked like diamonds hanging from above. "I'll be right up." She jogged up the marble steps of the grand staircase and was met at the top by Sebastian.

"This way." He led her into the rooms that he once

shared with his beloved Helena. "I have something to ask you, and if you don't approve then think nothing more of it."

"What is it, Sebastian?"

He motioned toward the huge, four-poster bed that used to be his. Her mouth fell open. There, laying across the bed, was the silk gown she first saw in the trunk in the attic. It appeared brighter, as if it had been cleaned. She looked from the dress to Sebastian.

"I would be honored if you'd wear it to the ball. Helena wore the gown when we wed. She would have adored you, and I know she would have loved you to wear it to the opening of our home."

Tears fell generously down Brynn's cheeks. "Oh, Sebastian."

"If you've something else picked out, I understand."

"I have nothing that would compare to the beauty of this dress, or this moment. I hope it fits."

"I took the liberty of finding your size and had Jax deliver it to a seamstress. He hasn't seen the dress, of course. I thought you'd like to make it a surprise."

"Oh, Sebastian. I'd hug you if I were able."

"There's no need for the waterworks. Dry your eyes. I have something else." He moved over to an ornately carved jewelry box. "Open it."

"Sebastian…"

"Go ahead."

Brynn lifted the lid, and caught her breath. "Are these diamonds?"

"Of course, they're diamonds. I was a wealthy man. Do you think I'd give Helena paste?" She would have laughed at his horrified expression if she hadn't been so overwhelmed.

"We'd need armed guards for me to wear this. I couldn't."

"You can, and you will. I believe your date would qualify as protection."

Her heart swelled, as it always did, with the thought of Jax. "I don't know…"

"You'll be the belle of the ball, my girl, just as it should be on your special day."

"It's our special day, Sebastian. I wish you could be there."

"Oh, I'll be there. I might be in the balcony, but I'll be there."

"Thank you. Not, just for this, but everything you've done for me. You have been my friend, my protector, and that parental voice I've needed at times."

"I am equally fond of you, Brynn. Now, I must be on my way. There are still plans to be made."

She smiled as he faded away.

Chapter Forty-Two

The day had arrived. They had hired outside help, as Sebastian had suggested. They were using the entire downstairs. The tables would be set up in the mammoth living room, with more in the ladies' drawing room. Brynn hadn't wanted to move the furniture back upstairs, but they would need the room. Now, that she was comfortably lodged in her own suite, her former bedroom was a dining room again, complete with the original table that had belonged to Sebastian and his wife.

The kitchen would rival any restaurant but was tastefully designed to fit the time period. Brynn had done that for herself. Her guests wouldn't be seeing it, but she would, and keeping the castle true to its time was important to her. The kitchen staff had been here since early morning, preparing appetizers, dinner, and desserts. The chef, who had become a dear friend, was from the pub, where she shared her first dinner with Jax. It was hard to believe so much time had passed, and she'd met so many great people from town. At any rate, she had been shocked and pleasantly surprised at his culinary background. He shooed her out of the kitchen and told her he had a few surprises up his sleeve.

The fireplaces were all stocked and providing the heat for the evening. She stood in the rotunda that would serve as the dance floor. It took her breath away. The chandelier sparkled down on the beautiful display below. The aroma of roses and carnations filled the air. It was perfect.

Brynn looked around. Funny. She hadn't seen Jax since early this morning. She giggled. Maybe he was trying to figure out how to put on his tuxedo. There was nothing left for her to do, but get ready. Sebastian had generously volunteered his room. And Brynn considered it his room. There would be no guests occupying Sebastian Morgan's suite. It would be off limits. She had it finished the way it was when he lived here with Helena. And when she showed it to him for the first time, she saw the emotion in his eyes. If ghosts could cry real tears, that would have been the moment.

A knock sounded from the closed door. Maybe it was Jax. She tightened her robe, and pulled open the door. "Lola? You told me you had to work." She hugged her friend tightly, and refrained from jumping with joy.

"I couldn't miss this, could I? It's one of the most important days of your life. A new beginning. And, hey, I might meet some rich guy who'll rock my world."

Brynn laughed. "Do you have a dress?"

"Yep, right here." Brynn, in her excitement, hadn't noticed the dress bag hanging over her arm.

"It'll be like old times. You can do my hair." The night would be perfect now.

They spent two hours, laughing, reminiscing, doing each other's makeup, and slipping into their gowns. It was then, that Brynn thought she should break the news to Lola. "You're going to think I'm crazy, but I have a friend here that might surprise you."

"Oh, yeah? This sounds promising. Do tell."

"He lived in this house a century ago." Lola's eyes widened, but she remained silent. "His name is Sebastian Morgan, and he built this castle."

"You're telling me, and expect me to believe, he lives here and he's your friend?"

"I know it's a stretch, but…"

"Brynn, come on."

"There's only one way to prove it to you."

"You're going to introduce me to a ghost?" Did the sarcastic tone in her voice hold a little fear?

"I am, but let's finish getting ready first. Help me into this dress?"

Lola zipped the back, and Brynn turned to face her. Tears fell down her friend's face, and she was a bit taken aback. Outward emotion wasn't Lola's thing. "You're crying? You're kidding me?"

"You look beautiful. You deserve so much happiness, Brynn. I'm happy I could be here to share this with you."

She smiled and hugged her friend. "Me too." Brynn faced the mirror, and she was pleased with the image that stared back at her. Her hair was done in a toned down version of an Edwardian hairstyle, piled on top of her head, with her natural ringlets hanging from the sides. It was a very feminine style that suited her. The dress hugged every curve and exposed a bit more than Brynn was used to, but this was the style of the time. The gold silk was covered with fine lace, and a small train flowed behind her. Brynn felt like a princess. Now, for the last piece.

Brynn opened the box, and Lola gasped. "Where

did you get that? And does he have a brother?"

"If he did, he's probably in the local cemetery. Sebastian gave me these to wear this evening. They belonged to his wife."

"Are those real diamonds?"

"Yes, my dear, they are very real." Sebastian spoke from the door. "Brynn, you rival my Helena's beauty. She would be proud."

"I don't know how to thank you."

"Be happy. That would be gratitude enough."

Brynn glanced at her friend. She'd forgotten this was her first encounter with the spirit world. Lola leaned against the wall, gaping openly. "Sebastian, I'd like to introduce you to my best friend from home. This is Lola."

"It's a pleasure to make your acquaintance, Miss Lola."

"You're a ghost?" The whispered sentence was barely audible.

"Some would say, yes."

From behind him, a woman spoke. "There has never been a more handsome man. I should never have let you get away."

A soft, sweet voice from the door grabbed everyone's attention. Brynn knew immediately it was Helena…

Chapter Forty-Three

Brynn's mouth gaped open now too. Helena Morgan was there, in the flesh. There was no misty apparition. Brynn could pinch her. She continued to watch as Sebastian's transformation occurred right before her eyes. Tears streamed down her face. She knew, without a doubt, this was his closure.

Sebastian scooped Helena into his arms. "Is it really you? Helena, I'm so sorry I didn't find you. I had no idea what happened. If only I'd read your journal all those years ago."

Helena smiled sweetly, and gently touched his face. "Tonight is for new beginnings, Sebastian, not old troubles. I doubted our love, and I paid the price. But now, we are together, and that's all that matters." She walked over to where Brynn stood in awe. "You must be Brynn. I am honored that you are wearing this gown on such an important evening. This is the gown I wed Sebastian. It's very special." Her kind face put Brynn immediately at ease. "There's someone who'd like to speak with you before you join the festivities."

Brynn gasped when Nate walked into the room. She bit down on her lip to fight the sobs that were rising to the surface. "No…it can't be…"

"Sebastian…Lola…let's leave them alone."

Brynn didn't even see them leave. She blinked furiously. This had to be some kind of dream.

He reached out and took her hands in his. She could feel his warm flesh. "Are you really here?"

"I am, but not for long, so I need to say a few things. I'm proud of you, Brynn. You put an end to my unfinished business. And look what you've done with our dream…you've made it a reality."

"Nate, I'm so sorry…I've betrayed you."

"No, Brynn. I'm not sorry. He's a good man, and he loves you the way I loved you. He'll make you happy."

She shook with emotion. "I still love you, Nate."

"I know, Brynn. What we had was ours, but it's time for you to move on. You have my blessing." He took the diamond necklace from the wooden box and fastened it around her neck. "You always were the most beautiful woman around. I've got to go, Brynn, but say yes tonight…yes, to happiness."

He kissed her softly on the cheek. The warmth of his lips against her skin was not her imagination. She closed her eyes, and opened them. He was gone.

The next voice she heard was Sebastian's. "Are you okay, my dear?"

"Was he really here?" Her eyes strained to see him through the tears.

"He was. Because of you, he's able to move on. It's time you did the same."

"And you…look at you…you're flesh and blood. I can hug you."

He held out his arms, and she walked into his embrace. "My dear child, I have grown to love you like my own. There's someone waiting for you downstairs. Would you allow me to escort you to your guests?"

Brynn glanced into the mirror and dabbed at her

eyes. "I would be honored."

"But the honor is mine." He held out his arm, and she looped hers through. Yes, she was ready for the festivities to begin, and she was ready to have no other at her side, besides Jaxson Maddox.

They exited the bedroom and walked around the balcony of the rotunda. The music of the orchestra played below, with the laughter and joy lifting to her ears. They descended the upper level of the grand staircase, with Sebastian stopping at the landing. Brynn looked down to find Jax waiting at the bottom step in his tuxedo. She inhaled sharply at the sight of him. She knew he was most comfortable in jeans and a t-shirt, but nothing prepared her for the prince that waited for her at the bottom of the stairs.

"Are you ready, my dear child?"

"Yes. I'm finally ready."

The orchestra played quietly in the background, and the guests gathered close by as she reached the bottom step. Sebastian removed her hand from the crook of his arm and placed her hand in Jax's. Brynn's eyes met Sebastian's with question. She didn't have to wait long for the answer. Jax dropped to one knee, with a diamond shining in his hand.

"Brynn, we've worked hard for tonight. This is our time to celebrate all we've accomplished, and the beginning of all we can accomplish. When you walked into my life, you brought me the other half of my heart. I never want to know what it feels like to be without it again. Marry me, Brynn Austin. Let's start our life together right now, in this moment."

The love between them overwhelmed her. If any doubt existed before she descended those stairs, it was gone. She knew what she wanted. She thought of Nate, and their conversation upstairs. Had it been real? Did he really give her his blessing? Something pulled her eyes to the back of the rotunda. There he stood, letting her know it wasn't her imagination. He nodded, a peaceful smile across his face.

Brynn focused all her attention on Jax, with a love that was finally free. "Yes, Jax, I'll marry you."

He lifted her from the step, and spun her around. "I was hoping you'd say that. There's no time like the present."

"What?" Her eyes widened.

"Welcome to your wedding." Lola hugged her. "You think I'd call off work for just a silly little dance? You needed a maid of honor, and I got the call."

Brynn shook her head in disbelief. Jax's mother stepped forward and embraced her. "I'm sorry we haven't gotten to know each other better before this, but we'll remedy that soon. My son loves you, and that's enough for us."

"Wow. When you ask someone to marry you, you mean business." A grin spread across her face. He was serious. They were going to be married, right here, right now. She had only one thing to add. "This night couldn't be more perfect for a wedding, but I have one request."

"Anything." Jax squeezed her hand.

"Sebastian, will you give me away?"

He moved from Helena's side against the wall, his shoulders back and proud. "I would like nothing more." Sebastian held out his arm, and for the first time she saw the glistening pride in his eyes.

Brynn put her arm through his, and faced forward.

The chairs were arranged in the rotunda for a wedding. Flowers were everywhere. "You've been doing a lot of planning I wasn't aware of."

"Some," he mused.

Romeo sprawled lazily across the piano. "That damned rodent hunter. I told him to wait upstairs."

Brynn laughed. "Look, he even wore his tuxedo." The black cat with the white fur across his chest—at one time, he was her only friend in town. "He deserves to be here."

She looked around at the guests assembled. All people she'd gotten to know since she arrived…people who'd welcomed her, and who she now called friends. The music began, and she took her first steps toward a new life.

****

The evening was like a fairy tale. She had married her prince and presided over the ball. She stood away from the guests, watching him with pride. He and Mike were sharing a laugh until he glanced in her direction. He walked toward her, and her heart sped with anticipation. He grabbed her hand and pulled her toward the doorway.

"Jax, we still have guests."

"I know, but we have some goodbyes to say."

His hesitation didn't give her a good feeling. When she walked through the door, she instantly knew it wasn't a temporary thing.

"I'm sorry, my dear, for dragging you away from your party. Helena and I wanted a word with you, before…"

"You leave." Brynn finished the sentence. "I should be happy for you both, but I'm more selfish than

I realized."

Helena moved forward first. Her dainty, glove-covered hands held tightly to hers. "Goodbyes are never easy. Of this, I know. I owe you so much. Without you, Sebastian may have never found out the truth and forgiven me, forgiven himself. We are going to have our happily ever after. Thank you, my dear." She kissed Brynn on each cheek and moved aside to give Sebastian his turn.

"You are the daughter I never had, my Brynn." His voice was thick with emotion. "It will be most difficult to leave you to your own devices, but I feel confident in my successor." He nodded in Jax's direction. "I promise we will meet again one day. I'll be waiting for you. In the meantime, enjoy your life, have lots of little ones, don't let them jump on my furniture, and take care of my home. It belongs to you now."

Brynn swiped at her face and held on tightly to Sebastian. She didn't want to let him go, but she knew she must. He had spent too many days in the darkness.

Sebastian opened the door to the solarium, and she and Jax followed. "Take care of my girl, Mr. Maddox."

"Count on it."

Off in the distance the night sky lit with brilliant colors. "Jax, do you think…?"

"They're going home? Yeah, Brynn, they're going home."

Wrapped in the warmth of her husband's arms, she watched Sebastian and Helena walk, hand in hand, toward the light. It was bittersweet, but she knew they would meet again. Sebastian Morgan was always true to his word.

A word about the author…

Lisa DeVore has always dreamed of being a published author since she wrote her first "book" at age eleven. Living in her NE Ohio town, with its own castle, led to an active imagination.

She splits her time between family, writing, and utilizing her accounting degree. She's an avid reader, loves dolphins, the beach, and hearing from her readers on Facebook or Twitter.

Lisa is married to her best friend, and they have two sons and a daughter.

~*~

Other Lisa DeVore titles
available from The Wild Rose Press, Inc.:

BEAUTIFUL MUSIC
ESCAPING CHRISTMAS
FACE THE MUSIC